ABOUT THE BOOK

The expert touch of master storytelling—entirely different from anything you have ever tried!

From **A. J. Payler**, master of modern fiction behind *The Killing Song, Bank Error in Your Favor*, and *Terror Next Door* comes *Stop All Interference*—seven stories of struggle against overwhelming odds and unstoppable fear, people pushed beyond betrayal and forgiveness, of the world we live in and what people will let themselves do just to survive in it.

Featuring:

"Sometimes, People Just Have Things They Have to Do": Everyone—*everyone* said that getting the Artery Boys back together was impossible… and once, high-powered music manager Alec Rodenbaugh might even have agreed. But nothing in this world is truly impossible for someone who wants it badly enough. And even if what seemed like the perfect cover might instead turn out to be the perfect crime… well, sometimes, people just have things they have to do.

"Default Admin Credentials": It seemed like the perfect crime… that should have been his first warning. Labor Day Weekend, an empty office building down in sleepy Point Loma: basically a sitting-duck target for any second-story man worth a nickel. Especially one with a lifetime of skills to draw upon—not to mention all the magic passcodes tucked comfortably away in his back pocket. Nothing could go wrong, or that was how it seemed… but in the end, he couldn't honestly blame anyone but himself for not seeing it coming.

"Sonata of Fear": When terror walks… no one is safe. Kenji Sanada has always been more comfortable with classic fictional monsters than with other people, even his family—Dracula, Frankenstein's monster, the mummy, all safely immortalized on his wall of fame. But what will he do when the all-too-real horrors of modern reality threaten to break right through those selfsame walls?

"The Rumble of Heat Lightning Above the Deep Midwestern Woods": A mysterious figure stalks the murky backwoods of the Midwest on an unrelenting mission for revenge, with nothing but a Bowie knife to protect him against the monsters that haunt the forest. And even if he's able to find what he needs… it's already too late.

Also featuring **"Dictated, Never Read"** (as seen in *Twenty-two Twenty-eight*), **"An Ideal for Living"** and **"Telemarketing in Reverse"**, available here and nowhere else.

OTHER BOOKS BY A. J. PAYLER

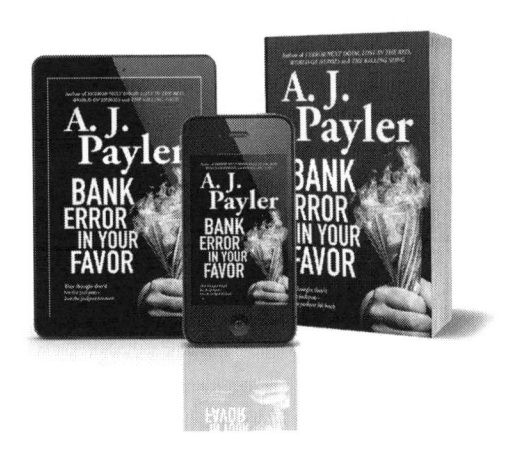

BANK ERROR IN YOUR FAVOR

What would you do if enough money to solve all your problems fell in your lap?

Shane and Jewel have been hanging onto the edges of life by their fingernails for so long, they can't remember any other way of living. When enough money to solve all their problems drops out of the sky, it seems like a windfall from heaven—but it might be the worst thing that could ever have happened.

Can love survive when money comes between lovers? Caught between the criminal underground and the law, Shane and Jewel race towards freedom despite a parade of bizarre characters, secret plans, and hidden agendas standing between them and the life they so desperately need. And worst of all, their greatest enemy of all might be looking back at them from the mirror—or right by their side.

https://books2read.com/bankerror

Terror Next Door

**Quarantined. Isolated. Paranoid.
TRAPPED.**

Stuck at home with nowhere to run, Kevin Tamura isn't holding up well under quarantine.

Exhausted from overwork and lack of sleep, his sanity slips as society crumbles.

But what will he do to protect himself when the greatest terror of all might be hiding right next door?

From the mind of A. J. Payler, author of *Lost In the Red* and *The Killing Song*, comes a story of a man pushed to the edge in a world that's ready to break.

Suffused with gripping tension, the explosive TERROR NEXT DOOR is a thrilling suspense novel no reader will ever forget.

https://books2read.com/terrornextdoor

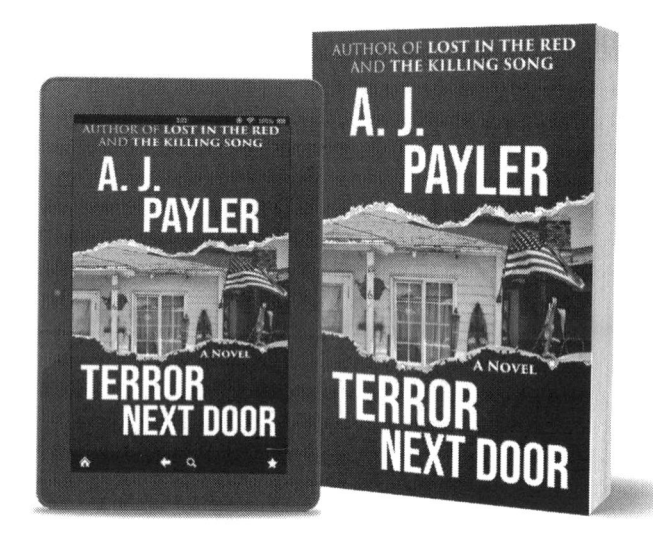

Lost In the Red

Out of their element—and trapped beyond time!

Carson Adkins had no doubt he was born unlucky, especially after his college folded one semester before graduation—but he never expected to find himself caught deep in the heart of an uncharted land sheltered against the passage of time for decades!

Compelled to struggle for survival against terrifying odds and unfamiliar threats, Carson finds himself in a world he never expected, where every encounter forces him to confront deadly opponents and difficult truths.

When the alluring Delilah Munson joins his journey, Carson believes he may finally have discovered something worth fighting for—but as he soon discovers, this opaque backwoods jewel has her own agenda, not to mention the will to carry it out.

Torn between two worlds, can the fragile yet ever-growing attraction between a rural princess and a modern man far from home possibly survive in the face of a cataclysmic conflict far beyond the bounds of anything either could ever have imagined?

THE KILLING SONG

1996, the American Midwest:

Zach Coleman is beginning to suspect the nineties aren't all they're cracked up to be. His fledgling private investigation career is sinking fast, his band just broke up, and even his boring day job isn't paying off.

But when a chance audition with a long-lost, legendary rock star leads to the opportunity of a lifetime, will Zach turn his back on everything he's known and pray both his worlds don't burn down around his ears?

A thrilling tale few will ever forget, this twist-filled narrative vividly resuscitates the smoke-saturated culture of the late nineties, smashes it up against the ruins of sixties radicalism, and gleefully deconstructs the remains into a thing of terrifying beauty.

https://books2read.com/thekillingsong

Get a free story when you sign up for the newsletter

Sign up for the A. J. Payler newsletter at http://ajpayler.com now to get the short story "Sonata of Fear" sent directly to you immediately, as well as receive future notifications of new releases.

Your email will not be shared with any other organizations or individuals, and you will not be barraged with marketing nonsense. Feel free to unsubscribe or resubscribe at any time; no one's feelings will be hurt. (Also, maybe check your junk/spam folder if you don't see the subscription confirmation with your free download link pop up relatively quickly.)

Visit ajpayler.com

Copyright © 2024 by A. J. Payler

All rights reserved. The moral right of the author has been asserted. No part of this book may be reproduced in any form or by any electronic or mechanical means, including information storage and retrieval systems, without written permission from the author, except for the use of brief quotations in a book review.

This is a work of fiction. Names, characters, places, and incidents either are the product of the author's imagination or are used fictitiously. Any resemblance to actual persons, living or dead, events, or locales is entirely coincidental. No generative large machine learning models ("AI") were used at any point in the composition of this work.

"Sometimes, People Just Have Things They Have to Do" originally published by Short Story (Substack), February 15, 2023. "Default Admin Credentials" originally published by Creepy Podcast, August 13, 2023. "Dictated, Never Read" originally published by Twenty-two Twenty-eight, June 30th 2023.

Original art elements: Jim Reilley (*The Perfect Crime* #19, Dec. 1951, "Murder Is Mad")

Cover and book design: A. J. Payler

STOP ALL INTERFERENCE

Stories

A. J. PAYLER

AJP

CONTENTS

Sometimes, People Just Have Things They Have to Do	13
Default Admin Credentials	31
Dictated, Never Read	39
Sonata of Fear	42
An Ideal for Living	54
Telemarketing in Reverse	59
The Rumble of Heat Lightning Above the Deep Midwestern Woods	64
Author's Note	93
Also by A. J. Payler	95
About A. J. Payler	97
Music by Aaron Poehler	99
The Killing Song	100
Lost In the Red	101
Terror Next Door	102
Bank Error In Your Favor	103

SOMETIMES, PEOPLE JUST HAVE THINGS THEY HAVE TO DO

Barton Nunez stared down at the table, fingertips of one hand idly tracing the ring where his water glass had rested while the other tugged compulsively at the ends of his thinning but still carbon black shoulder-length hair. His head hung low enough for Alec to see the white of Barton's scalp—maybe it was time to recommend one of those caps, the kind British rock stars who collected old cars always wore. Then again, Barton always looked uncomfortable in anything fancier than jeans and a t-shirt —he'd been fidgeting all evening inside the fashionable tailored suit required to fit in with the upscale dress code of Michel's on Main.

"But, I don't understand," Barton mumbled without looking up. "The show was sold out. Weeks in advance, even."

Suppressing the urge to allow his blue-grey eyes to roll to the back of his pristinely razor-cut ash-blond head, Alec Rodenbaugh sipped at his twenty-year-old tawny, doing his best to ignore the light piano jazz trickling down from the speakers concealed somewhere in the textured restaurant ceiling while he savored his digestif.

This was why he always waited until after dinner to break bad news. Otherwise, Barton would have whined and groused all through the meal, imploring Alec to appeal to some nonexistent higher power to somehow invalidate the incontrovertible truth he had called Barton to the finest restaurant in the county—by some assessments, at least—to confront him with. All that might have been accomplished would have been to spoil both of their meals; to ruin a dinner at Michel's would be a crime.

Besides, as Alec had often found occasion to muse to himself, he couldn't control much of anything, really.

Nor could anyone. But perhaps music managers were forced to face that fact more often than most, and thus came to live with it more readily than those who could afford to go on from day to day continually deluding themselves about the nature of the world they lived in.

After swallowing the last drops of the port wine he'd indulged himself in to finish off the dinner—it all got charged to expenses—he wiped his mouth, loudly smacking his lips to lift Barton's eyes from the resin-sealed table surface.

"It's simple," Alec said, struggling to keep his voice from sliding into the lecturing elementary-school teacher tone he used with his children. "Yes, the show last weekend at the Medina sold out. And sure, you managed to attract a full house for the debut of Pica Tontine. Even that god-awful opening band the club booker insisted on crowbarring onto the bill didn't drive anyone off before you played your set."

"Damn straight. We brought them out and packed the place to the rafters." Barton straightened his back, the faintest hint of a smile ghosting across his face. Poor sod was so desperate to salve his ego, he couldn't even tell when he was being set up for a fall.

"But," Alec continued, "between your first number and your final encore, you lost at least a quarter of the audience."

Barton winced. "That's not so bad," he claimed. "We played a long set. It was getting late. People just have things they have to do sometimes. Some of them probably had to get up early in the morning."

"On a Sunday?" Alec raised an eyebrow. "Come on, not your fans. Not many of them anyway."

"Well, all the real fans would have stuck around if they'd known we were going to wrap up with a few old Artery Boys favorites," Barton rebutted.

"Well, maybe you should have told them that before the encore, then," Alec muttered. "But either way, as you and I and your account manager down at the bank should all know, ultimately it all comes down to the numbers. And if the fans had as good a time as you seem to want to believe, they would have opened their wallets to prove it."

Barton stared back at him. "What does that mean?"

Alec sighed. "Look, I love the Medina, I know you love playing there. It's a great club, with a great sound system, it attracts a great crowd."

"But?"

"But part of what makes it so great is that it's severely limited in size. Sure, you attracted a capacity crowd, but let's be real, that's not really that hard to do there. Not for a longtime hometown favorite making a rare appearance in a smaller venue than fans are used to seeing him in. The bar makes their money off alcohol, but at twenty bucks a ticket with a legal capacity of two hundred and fifty, your end of the box office take only adds up so far."

And twenty percent of not much was practically less than nothing, Alec stopped himself from adding.

Barton's lips were a thin line. "Box office is only half the picture," he said. "Merch sales should help make up the rest—that's why we made those limited-edition shirts for the debut. Wasn't it?"

"It was," Alec confirmed, wincing sympathetically as he slid his credit card into the leather folder at the edge of the table. "And if they had sold like we were both hoping, we wouldn't be having this discussion right now."

His client's expression fell. Reality was starting to sink in, Alec saw.

"Oh," Barton said, finger now tracing the ring of condensation on the table in the opposite direction. "How bad was it?"

Alec paused, considering his options. He could soft-pedal his delivery, cushion the blow for Barton, preserve his old friend's feelings. Let him hold out hope for the continuation of Pica Tontine as a periodic side project, maybe on a regional tour of small venues.

But if Alec so did, it might be at the expense of their futures—all of their futures. Barton's, as a viable musical artist surviving on the creative output of his fevered mind. Alec's, as his manager, directing and shaping that output to maximize their collective capacity to stay housed and clothed and fed. Plus, there was Barton's family to think about, as well. Being out on the street wouldn't do any of them any favor.

"Put it this way," Alec said, winding up slowly to ensure the message was delivered in terms Barton would understand. "Allie Austin, with all her hits and awards and millions of social media followers, she makes around seventeen bucks a person at the merch table at every one of her shows. A long-running heavy rock band with a devoted following like Poison Flag or Heavy Light, you're talking in the neighborhood of twelve, thirteen dollars a person. Even a new group like Sayonara Mob can rack up eight or nine per capita if they're doing it right."

"So what did we do last night?" asked Barton, anxious for the other shoe to drop.

"Three," Alec said. "Three and a quarter. We even went a little light on pressing up the shirts hoping to create some false scarcity, but the booth didn't come close to selling out. There's a full box we had to stick back in the storage space, and they all have Saturday's date plastered across the back, so they're not even evergreen."

"Oh," Barton said, his voice small as realization began to sink in that the returns were in, with results nowhere near to what he'd hoped.

But Barton wasn't ready to give up the ghost of Pica Tontine yet. Alec could tell by the way the corners of Barton's jaw flared as he clenched his teeth, internally preparing his defense. He'd spent a full year getting the new band prepped, composing and discarding material, writing and rewriting possible set lists—he wasn't going to throw that all away on the basis of one bad night.

Not unless Alec fully impressed upon him the importance of doing so, anyway.

"Look," Barton said finally, winding up to deliver his defense at the same moment Alec spotted the waiter in the far corner giving them the peculiar stinkeye reserved for diners pushing up against the limits of outstaying their welcome at Michel's.

Alec shook his head. How things had changed. They never would have cared about a measly extra half-hour here or there back when Barton was riding high in the Artery Boys days.

But Barton didn't see it. "You're comparing apples to, I

don't know, kumquats," he ranted. "We don't play that slick commercial country pop like Allie Austin, she sells to moms and teenage girls and every song sounds like it could be in the background of a car commercial."

"That's true," Alec conceded. "Your music is nowhere near as commercial as hers, and never has been. No threat of that."

Brushing off the backhanded compliment, Barton barreled on. "And metal fans are crazy, they're only legendary for it. They're more than happy to have a full drawer packed with nothing but black print tees plastered with ugly-ass logos. Sayonara Mob? Those posers are just surfing the wave of hip appeal and making that money off gullible college kids while it lasts. In a year, they won't be able to give that junk away."

"Fine, then," Alec said, having fully anticipated Barton's response—hell, he'd practically teed him up for the killing blow. "Let's compare kumquats to kumquats then. Two years ago, on what you called the 'final' Artery Boys tour, you were pulling in an average of seven-fifty a night in merch sales per person. And back then, you guys were playing places six, eight, sometimes ten times the size of the Medina. We're never going to have a promotional hook like the new band's first show, so realistically speaking, Saturday's numbers represented a peak, not an anomaly. I mean, come on, Barton—you do the numbers."

Barton fell silent. That was math he couldn't argue with; that tour had been the source of the nest egg on which he and his family had lived since the demise of the Artery Boys, keeping the lights on while he strived towards getting his new project off the ground.

But now it seemed that Pica Tontine might never get its chance to soar, instead crashing upon takeoff.

"So what are you saying, then, Alec? That I should

make up with that asshole Nico? Play nice, get the Artery Boys back together and strum a few tunes with a guy like him?"

Barton stood and threw his napkin to the table dramatically. In the corner, the waiter half-lurched forward, but relaxed when he saw Barton sit back down again.

"And I can't believe you of all people would ask that of me. You know who he is, who he really is, and what he did. What he's done, and will continue to do. I mean… how can you even ask that of me, knowing what he's like?"

Alec carefully set his crumpled linen napkin on the table surface, nodding to the waitstaff to signal their intention to depart presently. Judging from the present intensity of the disapproving glares they were receiving, whoever had the ten o'clock seating reservation for their table was almost certainly cooling their heels in Michel's lobby presently.

"I'm not telling you to do anything except what's best for you and your career," Alec said, standing from the table and brushing down the front of his shirt. "Hell, I'm not telling you to do anything. That's not my role, and never has been. You make the decisions; I make the calls."

Barton stood, reluctantly. "That's right. It is my career, after all."

"Right," said Alec. "But I can tell you the calls for the Artery Boys come with a lot higher price tags attached than those for Pica Tontine ever will, especially after Saturday night. You think venue owners don't talk? Gossip with each other about what band drew what crowd and what band didn't? Word gets around, and it gets around fast."

"Sure, of course," Barton admitted, reluctantly dragging himself to his feet as the waiter over in the corner champed at the bit to turn the table over. "But it was just one night," he said, powerful baritone voice now drained of its vigor.

Alec shook his head. "I know, buddy—but it was the one night that counted."

Barton held his head in his hands. "Christ. I can't believe I'm even sitting here seriously thinking about this. If the fans knew what Nico was really like, no one would fault me for not wanting to work with him again. I mean, I know what they say, addiction is a disease, hate the sin not the sinner, all that shit—but fuck, man. He fucking gave that shit to my little brother, Alec, you know he did!"

Eyes wide, Alec placed a finger to his lips. "You know why you can't talk about that publicly."

"I know, I know," Alec grumbled, waving his hand. "Goddamn it, you don't have to remind me, of all people."

"Well, good," Alec said. "Just so long as we're all still keeping our heads on straight, no matter the circumstances."

"If only…" Barton said, now staring at the ceiling, all thoughts of departure from Michel's clearly forgotten. "If only there was some way to do it and cut Nico out. Bring the Artery Boys back without the cancer that killed the band in the first place."

"Right, well, that's all nice to think about," Alec said. "But as long as he holds the trademarks on the name and ancillary branding, you come within fifty yards of any of that and the lawyers will have us shut down before you sing one note. And you know all this, so why are we even talking about it?"

Barton banged his fist flat on the table suddenly. "Damn it, you know he stole all that right out from under the rest of us. And stealing the name doesn't even make the top ten of his most egregious offenses. I can't, I just… I can't even think about it."

At the impact of Barton's fist on the table Alec couldn't help feeling acute awareness of the circular perimeter of annoyed and concerned glances surrounding them; he waved to the servers to indicate both his apology and intention to clear the table as soon as he was able. That was a lot to put on one feeble flip of the hand, though, and Alec felt their time running short.

"You know what would be best for everyone," he heard Barton say, quietly, as if speaking more to himself than his manager and friend. "If he was dead."

"Don't say that," Alec said. "Not even joking. He was your friend once. And mine."

"That was a long time ago," Barton pointed out correctly. "And if you really thought about it, all things considered, you'd know what I said is true. We could get the rest of the band back together free and clear, bring in any of a dozen dependable pros to cover the bass slot, head back out on the road tomorrow. Hell, even the fans would get what they wanted—the band back together, and a chance to say goodbye to the Nico they think they know. The idea of what he maybe once represented, but hasn't come close to in real life in longer than I can remember. Tell me that doesn't sound good?"

Alec bit his lip. "I can't," he said. "But if we don't clear this table in the next fraction of a second you and I are going to be the ones whose lives are at risk. Come on," he said, beckoning his rambling client to follow. "This is why we planned ahead and took rideshares instead of driving ourselves. Let's head over to the Dawnbreak, get a couple more drinks, see if anyone interesting is playing tonight."

"No," Barton said, slurring his words as he pushed

away from his seat. "You go on if you want, I'm done for the night."

For a moment, Alec fought his instinct to argue with Barton, to harangue him to come out and party like the old days.

But it was better this way, with Barton heading back home. He wasn't so drunk he wouldn't think long and hard about the choices to be made, what he'd have to to get back where they needed to be.

It was simple math, really. They needed Barton's talent, plus the Artery Boys name. Nico owned part of the name, but with the way Barton felt about the drugs that were woven into the very fabric of the life Nico led, Barton would never speak to him, let alone work with him again.

So something had to done to solve the equation, make the variables add up differently. That was all; nothing more than Alec was used to handling as a routine part of his managerial duties. It was what he did: manipulate situations in such a way that they worked out the best for his clients, and therefore himself.

That was all he'd done here, nothing more. And even if Barton hadn't agreed to it yet, at least now Alec knew the idea was rattling around in his head. When he got up in the clear light of day and he saw it was the best path for everyone, then things would start rolling, and fast.

Sitting in the back of the rideshare on his way back to his apartment, Alec stared idly out the window watching the lights of North County fly by. Ten years ago, he'd barely ever needed to come this far north—back then, everything worth his attention was within a few miles of the downtown area. The Gaslamp, the Medina, all the best restaurants. North County was for the horse races and startup companies and endless suburbs full of retirees, and not much else.

But things were changing. San Diego County was big—one of the biggest in the country—and both restauranteurs and venue owners had largely fled the downtown, leaving it to the hordes of unhoused and addicted roaming the tight grid at the heart of the city. Now, you could get the best Asian food outside of Tokyo right in Kearny Mesa, of all places, a neighborhood once best known for car dealerships and chain stores. What difference did location make when half of an eatery's clientele sat on their butts at home and had delivery drivers bring their food to them?

He shook his head. Getting people out, whether to see a show or eat a meal, had never been easy. But it seemed to be getting harder and harder every year. And you couldn't ship the concert experience to someone's home the way you could a bowl of tonkotsu chashu ramen or a plate of spicy shrimp dumplings.

They'd tried, of course. During the pandemic, Barton had consented to a couple of ticketed livestreams—special advance previews of what was to come with his new band, as they'd billed them. But with the group playing on an empty stage, the conclusion of each unfamiliar song fading off into endless empty silence instead of buried in the rush of applause, it made the whole thing feel antiseptic and bloodless.

At the time, he'd told both Barton and himself that things would be different once they were able to get back to doing what Barton did best—pump up a crowd live and in person. As a tunesmith, Barton was maybe one in a thousand, charitably speaking. But as a frontman, he was one in a billion, every minute move enrapturing his awestruck fans and overwhelming them with raw charisma.

Or at least that was the way it was when Barton was with Artery Boys. On his own, it seemed the case was not as certain. And whatever Barton wanted to portray by billing Pica Tontine as a band of equals, in the eyes of most it was very much considered the new project by the guy from Artery Boys—and that was the sole criterion by which it would either rise or fall.

It was a delicate balance, Alec knew. The type of self-assurance necessary to be a great frontman depended on a combination of so many factors—musical skill, performing ability, audience resonance—that finding them all in a single person was as rare as striking a vein of gold in one's own backyard. When things were clicking, Barton's empathetic ability to sense what the audience was feeling, amp it up, and feed it right back to them was up there with the best.

He bit his lip. What if the problem wasn't Pica Tontine?

What if they got the Artery Boys back together—and they still didn't have it?

He shook his head. No, no. Whatever it was Barton had, it wasn't the kind of thing that went away like that.

He'd see. With or without Nico, they could get the Artery Boys' name back up on local marquees tomorrow, if they wanted. Even at a big place like the Palladium, downtown—the punters would still come down there for a big enough attraction. And San Diego didn't have a much bigger attraction to offer than the Artery Boys.

Hopefully, Barton would see it the same way.

"Here you go, chief," the rideshare driver drawled, pulling his anonymous sedan to the curb outside Alec's towering apartment building.

Alec rated the driver five stars and gave a generous tip before stepping out of the car. If he was rating honestly, he would have given three stars at best given the half-hour plus it had taken him to make what should have been a twenty-five minute ride at most—but it wasn't worth the hassle of risking his own app rating being honest just to prove a point.

Before he could place one foot on the curb, his phone started ringing. The display read 'San Diego Police Department,' and Alec's tongue was suddenly dry in his throat.

"Hello?" he asked, somehow knowing exactly what they were going to tell him before he'd even opened the line.

But it was still surprising to hear them say Nico was dead.

Up in his apartment, Alec's head whirled with a wild diversity of speculation and conjecture.

The buzz of the lobby intercom breaking him from his delirium, he realized he had the fingernails of one hand between his teeth—a habit he'd struggled mightily as a child to break.

Wiping his hand on his pants, he stepped over to the intercom plate mounted on the wall by the front door.

"Yes?" he asked, voice strained and foreign-sounding in his throat.

"Alec, buddy—let me up!" he heard from the crackly speaker, and then a sound he hadn't heard in some time, longer than he even realized—Barton's whoop of pure joy.

With a sigh, he pressed the buzzer and was swiftly rewarded with the familiar thud-thud-thud of Barton bounding up the staircase to the third floor two steps at a time, each heavy footfall resonating through the substructure of the building itself.

Within less than a minute, Barton was at his apartment building's entry.

"Ding dong, the witch is dead," he exclaimed, a grin plastered across his face. And plastered was definitely the right word.

"Goddamn it," Alec muttered, waving him to silence and ushering him inside before the neighbors overheard any more evidence worth passing along to San Diego's finest. At this rate, Barton was going to get them both arrested, maybe even that very night.

After all, the two of them had already been heard arguing loudly in public about how great it would be if he was dead. And not more than an hour later, the man's recently deceased corpse is discovered? Still warm, the policeman on the phone said. Alec wasn't a criminologist; he didn't even like those kinds of TV shows or podcasts. But you didn't have to know much to know the circumstances didn't look good, either for Alec or his client.

His client. Nico had been his client once, too. The three of them, tight, together, bound by trust.

A trust that would be their undoing. And ultimately, he supposed, led to at least one of their deaths.

Maybe more.

Barton burst into the room then, arms wide, each clutching a bottle of sparkling bubbly wine—nothing that could legally be called champagne, but drinkable all the same. One was mostly drunk already, in fact.

Barton pointed at Alec. "Alec, old pal, old buddy... did you hear?"

He nodded. "The police just called and told me. I can't believe it. It's such a shock."

"I know, right? We were literally just talking about it, and here the guy ends up found dead not more than an hour later. That's some spooky stuff."

"Weird coincidences happen all the time," Alec pointed out. "Besides, you and I both know Nico tended to maintain a wide variety of unsavory habits even at his best. Any one of those could have caught up with him at any time. It's a miracle something like this didn't happen earlier."

Barton grimaced. "Well, the prick didn't get voted Artery Boy most likely to die young for nothing,"

"True," Alec admitted. "And at least now you can proceed with a clear conscience and a legal claim, since all rights to the name revert to you instantly on his death."

"God, Alec," Barton said. "I can't think about that now."

But Alec could tell he was already.

Barton cocked his head, squinted at Alec.

"Hey… between you and me, Alec… you can tell me straight. Did you have anything to do with this? The, the coincidental timing? Because… I mean, it's hard to argue things work out way better for both of us this way, no?"

Alec struggled not to smile. "Of course not, Barton," he said. "I mean, didn't the police tell you? He shot up some bad skag, that's all. Occam's razor, the simplest solution is usually the right one."

Barton nodded. "Sure, sure. That makes sense. But usually isn't always. And the thing is, something that evidently you didn't know apparently, is that Nico's clean."

Alec's mouth was suddenly dry.

"Come on, Barton. Nico? Clean?" He forced a scoff, hoping to sound carefree, but it came out more of a dry croak. "I'm going to have to ask to see the receipts on that one."

Barton tucked a strand of his long dark hair behind his ear, folded his arms. "Yeah, he came to me awhile ago actually, as part of the whole making amends part of the process. He got clean the hard way, and stayed that way.

For eighteen full months. It took a year before I agreed to talk to him, but I'm glad I did."

"Wow," Alec said, shaking his head. "That makes it even sadder. A relapse like that, after so much success. Damn, that's just tragic."

"Yeah," Barton said. "Or it would have been, if Nico hadn't built up the willpower to know something was odd about all his old shooting buddies suddenly coming around and knocking on his door again, all trying to sell him on this new stuff some guy they'd never seen before gave them practically free.

Alec swallowed. "That right?"

Barton nodded, a smirk creasing his features. "That's right. Turns out Nico was clean enough that he had enough willpower to turn down week after week of hardcore party offers—a super shitty thing for a person to do to anyone, by the way, let alone a recovering addict. Eventually he figured out something had to be behind all of it and went to the cops, who it turns out are big Artery Boys supporters. Who the fuck knew, right?"

"Who could have predicted it," Alec concurred.

"So they requisitioned all the security footage in Nico's neighborhood for the last two months. And they found something funny, Alec. Something that looked a lot like you, or someone else with the same ash-blonde hair and the same hundred-dollar razor cut. Not a lot of guys that look like you running around Nico's area, I shouldn't have to tell you."

Alec turned to rush to the window, but he could hear the sirens from down below already. Barton must have raced like a maniac to get over here ahead of them.

"Since they were on the lookout," Barton continued, "they caught the guy you sent to set him up with a hot shot in a hot minute. By the way, where the fuck did you hire that asshole, Craigslist? He stuck out like a soccer mom at a Poison Flag show. And he talked just about as much, too. Once they got him in that little room, that is."

"Barton," Alec pleaded. "Come on, man. I did it for us."

"You did it for you," Barton said. "There never was an us. Like you said, you work for me—the only us is the band. Oh, and that reminds me, Alec—you might be interested to know that once I agreed to hear Nico's apology, he told me something interesting."

There was a blur of Barton's fist crashing into Alec's jaw, then his vision exploded in stars and he fell back against the wall, face contorted in pain.

"It was you all along, Alec. You thought Nico would be easier to control if he was hooked, and you thought the same thing about my brother too. And now, all the rotten shit you tried is coming back on you. But hey, look at it this way: you got your wish. The Artery Boys are back together, and it's all thanks to you. Nico and me are going to play the fucking Palladium and make us all a shitton of cash—and you'll be rotting in jail, not touching a penny of it. Plus now I can hire a better, more professional manager for five percent less than you took. So thanks for that, bro."

The police were stomping up the steps at the front of the building now, jabbing at the buzzer for the manager to let them in.

Barton smiled. "It took me some convincing for them to let me rush over just to be here to see your face when you realized just now badly you got fucked and see if I could get you to hang yourself even more than you already have, but like I said—you wouldn't believe what huge Artery Boys fans they are down there. Once I promised them all free seats for the Palladium show, they even volunteered to set you up perfectly by calling to give you the news about Nico's 'tragic death.'"

There were heavy footfalls in the hall outside, and pounding on his door, and Alec knew he wouldn't be seeing the Artery Boys reunion in person.

Hopefully they'd pay to have it professionally recorded, get a quick product out there to satisfy the instant demand their reunion and the scandalous circumstances around it would create for the group. But those kinds of decisions were no longer his purview.

He smiled even as the doorframe splintered and a contingent of leather and Teflon-clad centurions barreled through.

The funny thing was, even knowing how it turned out he wouldn't have done anything differently. Sure, not everything had worked out perfectly—it'd sting not being there to witness the band's rebirth in person—but he'd managed to get the band back together. No one could take that away from him, no matter what happened to him after that.

Sometimes, people just have things they have to do.

DEFAULT ADMIN CREDENTIALS

People argue about how complex passwords should be. But the truth is, it makes a lot less of a difference how a password is changed than whether anyone ever actually bothers to get around to changing it.

Most people would be amazed to know what percentage of computer systems never get their passwords changed. It changes from industry to industry, but not as much as you'd think, hovering somewhere between a third and a half across the board, even in high-tech fields where the people involved should—and definitely do—know better.

Kind of shocking, right? Routers, switches, mainframes, entire networks. Pretty much any and every crucial piece of the entire telecommunications backbone, basically all running on the default credentials they shipped with for years at a time.

And these default admin credentials, the magic passwords that let anyone access and mess around with the guts and internal working of the thing, you can look them up online without ever having to buy a piece of equipment. Check it out for yourself.

So if you do your homework and you can find out the make and manufacture of any given system, you have a damn fair shot at a butter-smooth entry without even a whiff of risk. It doesn't matter much whether a company manufactures soft drinks, builds military kit, or designs networking technology, if you can find out what make of equipment they use and finagle a means of uninterrupted access to said equipment, at least half the time plugging in the preconfigured default setup password will give you full admin privileges.

The best part is, ninety-nine-point-nine percent of the time you can count on the fact that the type of person who doesn't bother changing their passwords on one system never bothers to change their passwords anywhere. So once you find a viable target, it's generally safe to assume whatever systems they have access to are similarly undefended: security cameras, alarms, even personal email. 'Hacking' a password like you see in the movies and on television—random guessing at birthdays, hobbies, childhood pets, even unconnected objects around the room—is never necessary and doesn't work like that anyway, because someone too lazy to change the admin keypass for their multi-thousand security system is the same person who keeps their computer login on a sticky note under the keyboard.

If you're one of these people, take solace in the fact that you shouldn't blame yourself. It's just human nature, and believe me, you aren't alone by a long shot. We all imagine our friends, neighbors, and enemies are vigilant about keeping responsible practices, but for the most part they're all just like you.

Anyway, all this is taking the long way to getting

around to explaining how I ended up in the situation I got myself into this Labor Day weekend.

The Wiltshire Building is a squat, ungainly three-story painted slate gray, situated on the corner of a couple of glorified back alleys down in the industrial section of San Diego's Point Loma neighborhood. Point Loma itself is a peninsula, so access in and out of the place is limited to a couple of major roads and traffic tends to slow to a crawl whenever anything of note happens there—which is why I thought an overcast Labor Day would be the perfect time to finally get around to breaking into the offices of Carillion Industries, a four-room arrangement on the Wiltshire Building's second floor. A day with no business meant no traffic, no interruptions, and no risk. In and out in an hour or less and no one gets hurt, least of all me. It seemed perfect.

Unfortunately, that's not the way it worked.

Oh, I got past the office building security system without a hitch—it was old and unpatched and vulnerable to about seven different strategies—and rode the elevator straight up to Carillion's front door. Their keypad was a different make than that of the building itself but offered no greater challenge, so I was in their lobby within five minutes and had their security cameras shut down within ten.

For the next half-hour I scrounged through the front of the Carillion offices, ball cap screwed down tight on my head to keep from leaving any stray hairs for the authorities to test my DNA and shade my face from any backup cameras I might have missed, latex gloves keeping my fingerprints from any of the surfaces I touched, sunglasses on to hide my eye color and so forth. You know, the usual routine.

A couple of petty cash boxes scavenged from bottom

desk drawers added up to about five thousand in legal tender stuffed into the pockets of my workman's jumpsuit —always dress like you might have some legitimate excuse to be on the property, plus a jumpsuit covers a lot of potentially identifying marks—so I was pretty happy with the day's take before even getting into the back offices.

What I should have done at that point was to cut my losses, turned around and left both the office and building and driven right the fuck out of Point Loma right then. I would have been coming out five grand ahead and run almost zero risk of being caught.

But then I turned a corner, looked through a thick glass door and realized that behind the expansive black walnut desk in the CEO's office, there was a safe set into the wall.

And not just any random wall safe, but a Kroll-Siemens 480, recognizable by its distinctive hexagonal profile. Infamous in certain circles for its many, many design flaws, which made it only slightly more protection than just leaving your valuables in a mound in the middle of the floor.

Now, in retrospect, I should have been suspicious there was nothing obscuring the face of the safe, piece of junk or not. I mean, even the dumbest uppity prick hangs a self-aggrandizing portrait or a blowup of their boat or some ugly painting he paid too much for on the wall to conceal a safe, right? But okay, I missed that in my zeal to find out just what that Kroll-Siemens 480 might contain. No one could blame me for that.

The same admin passkey that opened the Carillion front office door unlocked the touchpad protecting the CEO's inner sanctum, no muss no fuss. Before you could say payday, I had my ear pressed to the safe, tapping around its edges to see what she had to tell me. And baby, it was a lot—this model hadn't even been upgraded in accordance with the recall Kroll-Siemens was forced to send out after the depths of their incompetence became known. That meant all it would take to pop the door was a flathead screwdriver applied in just the right spot, and the multi-tool I always kept hooked to my belt while on the job gave me three different flatheads on command.

So here's the thing: in my line of work, if you get past three different security hurdles to get access to a thing without trouble, that tends to set a pattern, right? It lulls you into a state of arrogance, like you can do whatever you want to people too stupid to take the most basic precautions to protect themselves.

You get lazy, is what I'm saying. And that's what happened here.

I mean, some rich asshole has a nonupgraded Kroll-Siemens 480 set into his wall, to me and others like me that's just asking to be robbed. And I guess that's what the idea was there, now that I put it all together: to create the image of an irresistible target, paint the picture of a sitting duck, in such a way that only a person with my specialized knowledge would recognize it. And why would anyone do something like that? The only reason would be to draw that person in.

I recall thinking, just before popping the face off the safe, that I had no idea what the hell business Carillion Industries was even in. Real estate? Bail bonds? Financial services? Who the hell knew? The name was vague enough that it could imply anything and everything or nothing at all, all at the same time.

I wasn't even sure how the place had gotten on my radar, not entirely. There are a few deep web bulletin boards where people like me buy, sell, and trade information about potential jobs, targets, and the like, so chances were solid I must have run across it there.

But I knew I hadn't paid for the tip, so it couldn't have been too carefully vetted. These websites are obscure, sure, but I don't fool myself they're secure enough that the cops and other miscreants don't know about them.

As I applied pressure with my multi-tool, I felt the face of the safe about to give way. The muscles in my shoulders tensed unconsciously, bracing for the piercing squeal of an alarm as it popped loose and came off in my hands—but there was nothing.

I grinned, tossing the face aside carelessly. With the entire guts of the lock mechanism exposed, even a toddler could open the thing in less than a minute; just click the tumblers into place, turn the handle, and blammo. That was why Kroll-Siemens paid out big bucks in their settlement, that was why anyone who was serious about trying to protect their belongings had long since gone back for the upgrade.

I was no toddler, so I had the door wide in a few seconds.

As I reached my hand inside, the hairs on the back of my neck stood on end. I shrugged it off as the thrill of the moment, the excitement of the hunt.

That wasn't it at all though, I now realize. It was my instincts, screaming at their lungs to try to warn me off at the last minute. Too late.

My fingers tripped some kind of laser sensor—or heat sensor, or movement sensor, one of those—situated inside the safe. Now, such a thing isn't unheard of, but in a place sloppy enough to have default credentials as issued on all their systems and a piece of crap wall safe? No one would expect it there.

I certainly didn't. And that's what they were counting on.

The office door behind me slammed shut with a hydraulic crash, a battery of resolute thunks signaling deadbolts sliding home into the walls all around me: the door, the windows, even the drawers of the desk itself. All secured firmly, with me still standing there with my hand in the otherwise empty safe and my dick in my hand, figuratively speaking.

My chin sagged to my chest, and I knew I was caught.

For the next half hour I checked and double-checked and triple-checked every opening, every lock, every crevice, from the sealed industrial triple-pane windows to the two-inch diameter ventilation shafts to the less than sixteenth-inch gap between door and threshold. I even pulled off the electrical plates, probing around the walls for weak spots in the drywall.

But in my heart I knew I wouldn't find anything, no matter how hard I looked. Mostly I just had to satisfy myself because I wouldn't have been able to forgive myself for not trying if I hadn't at least made the attempt.

But as expected, my search came up empty. There was no way out of this room, and I had the expertise to know that for certain as an irrefutable fact, as sure as up was up and down was down.

That was how they caught me, playing to that knowledge. When the mind knows a thing, it yearns to exercise that knowledge, to show off what it knows, try to distinguish itself above the pack. It's just human nature.

And there, trapped alone in the aridity of that solitary office with nothing to do but think, it came to me where the Carillion info came to me from. It was in a file I kept on my laptop in my apartment, containing information I'd dug up and cobbled together—and yes, sometimes even paid for—regarding potential targets, jobs I might undertake in the future. You can't just rely on waiting for things to drop in your lap, not if you want to maintain any semblance of a regular cash flow. You never know when you might need a bunch of money all of a sudden, after all. So a guy in my position has to always be tossing around somewhere between a few and a few dozen possibilities.

I didn't consciously recall putting that Carillion data in there, but I guess I must have assumed I copied it in there late one night after having a few strong double IPAs and tossing back a few gummies. It wouldn't be the first time I woke up to information in my job file I didn't consciously remember putting in there, though admittedly most of that type of info usually turned out to be irrelevant garbage.

Now, what I think is someone planted that information there to lure me. Knowing it would float to the top of my queue by presenting a target too tempting to resist. Or at least for a guy like me to resist.

I couldn't help kicking myself. All I would have had to do to prevent this would have been to change the default admin credentials on my laptop, the way I had on my modem and router. One weak link in the chain, one tiny oversight, and I was lost.

Now, I have no options left to me but to sit here slumped in this not-as-plush-as-it-looks office chair, staring out the unbreakable windows waiting for the blinding San Diego sun to come up, all the while wondering what type of person whoever eventually comes to get me might be, and what someone smart enough to pull this off could possibly want with a guy like me.

My guess is, there's no way it's anything good.

DICTATED, NEVER READ

It was a beautiful Sunday morning, shimmering rays of perfect golden sunlight reflecting placidly off the as-yet unbroken surface of the isolated mountain lake. The owls and chittering insects of the night had already retreated to their dens, all the night's hunters bedded down, relinquishing the day to the flora and fauna of morning—a decidedly more peaceful, soothing time.

Aerendyl Kiyama stretched her willowy limbs as her burnt umber eyelids fluttered open, greeting the arrival of the day—but not just any day, no. This was a special day, the day of her oh for fucksake you dumb asshole, please do the rest of us the favor of paying just the slightest bit of attention where you're going.

Oh Jesus, now look at this prick. Just take all day why don't you, it's not like anyone has anywhere to be at seven oh three on a Monday, yes surely we're all just cruising around downtown gawking at the skyscrapers like we just fell off the turnip truck and have never seen buildings taller than three stories before.

Yes yes, I see you, just move out of the way please.

All right, fucking finally. Where the shit was I? Oh right, the day of reckoning. So yeah, um, not just any day, this day of reckoning was one Aerendyl knew without a doubt she would ah, fuck! Jesus that's hot, where the hell are those napkins I stuffed down the console for emergencies just like this?

Ow ow ow ow ow. Oh man, this skirt is ruined. I knew wearing this shade of beige was a mistake on a day like today. Look at that, that's gonna sting later. And just great, now I don't have any coffee left either. Lovely.

So. Right. This day was one that would decide her future, to finally resolve whether Aerendyl would be allowed to pursue the path of the warrior—a desire all knew had long burned in her breast, to avenge the untimely death of her older brother Raloto—or if she would be consigned to the distaff lodge, there to dedicate herself to the perfection of the domestic arts.

Aerendyl shuddered, knowing she would be a different person by the time night again fell and the hunters of the forest roamed once more. Or would she, in fact, be the person she always had been as well as the person she was always meant to be?

Oh, what is this now. Ugh, are you serious? Fine, fine, pick up. Pick up!

Hello. What is it?

No, really, mother—I'm on my way to the office, I don't —all right, all right, fine. Good morning. How are you. I am fine. Now, what is it?

Oh, please. You call out of the blue during literally the only nineteen minutes of time I have to myself the entire f-ing day and then you dither around, I'm sorry, but yes, I'm going to tend to be blunt. I apologize.

Now will you please tell me why you—oh.

Well, why didn't you—no, I see.

Yes, I'm sorry, I'm sorry, I already said—yes, of course, I will.

Okay. Yes. Okay. I'll talk to you later.

Bye, mom. I love you.

Fuck.

Um. Aerendyl, um, Aerendyl stared at the water.

It, um.

Fuck.

SONATA OF FEAR

Outside, the storm beat furiously against the house's siding, causing it to rattle and shake with every gust.

Inside, Kenji shivered and pulled his thick robe tighter around him, clutching his steaming mug of hot chocolate tightly with both hands, as if the wind might break through the window behind him and tear it from his grasp.

He chuckled at himself. It was hard to shake the primitive instincts passed down through millions of years of evolution—early humans must have quaked in fear at every thundercrack as if they signified the rage of an angry god, rather than colliding fronts of air. But he was safe, he told himself; the storm was outside, where it belonged, and he was securely ensconced in his warm, comfortable den, surrounded by the accumulations of a life of fandom.

He looked up, smiling at the row of expensive collective figurines, one representing each of the classic monsters of film. The set was his prize possession, each one meticulously carved, cast in genuine bronze, and hand-painted by talented artisans until they seemed to glow with interior life, somehow even more vivid than the moving images of the characters they represented.

Frankenstein's monster glowered down at him stolidly, his bride by his side. Dracula peered through his cape as if waiting for an opportunity to strike. The mummy, the werewolf, the gill man—all there, frozen in place.

The only thing missing, he thought, chuckling to himself as he sipped at his mug, was an invisible figurine. Perhaps he should have left an empty space atop the bookcase and told people that was what it was—but then, no people other than his brother ever entered his den. Even their parents stayed out: Mom said the posters gave her nightmares, Dad just rolled his eyes and groaned at what he said represented a massive waste of money and time.

They didn't get it. No matter; Kenta did. It was the one thing the brothers always agreed on, even as their opinions diverged in nearly every other aspect: monsters were cool.

Kenta.

Kenji shook his head. He hoped his brother hadn't gotten in over his head this time. Federal agents calling meant he'd stumbled into something beyond Kenji's comprehension, or inclination at least—he preferred to leave politics to the politicians, whereas his brother was out marching every other week for one cause or another.

And now the repercussions of his actions were knocking on their family's front door. Figuratively, of course—a video call was hardly indicative of an imminent arrest or detainment—but from the way Mom had reacted to the news, you would have thought her oldest was about to be hauled off to the selfsame detention camps their great-great uncle had been forced into back in World War II.

He nearly dropped his hot chocolate at the shock of the ring announcing their call, somehow louder than the thunder outside.

Just breathe, he told himself. Just relax and tell them the truth. None of us have anything to worry about if you just chill out, tell them as little as possible of what Kenta really talks about, and they'll go away satisfied, and this whole thing will blow over. Then we can all go back to normal life, the way it was before.

His heart in his throat, he clicked the 'accept call' button on the laptop open on the desk before him.

The screen popped to life, displaying an image of two white men sitting side-by-side: one older, with a sharp widow's peak hairline and deeply etched lines around the corners of his mouth; one younger, his close-cropped hair still dark brown, his cheeks full and eyes bright with enthusiasm.

"Good afternoon," Kenji enunciated, leaning closer to the computer so his words would be clearly audible.

"Is it?" said the older man.

"Um," stumbled Kenji, already at a loss for words.

The older man gestured vaguely towards the background behind Kenji. "I just meant it seems like you're suffering some inclement weather there."

"Ah," Kenji said, the thunder cracking as if to punctuate the meaninglessness of his reply. "Yes. I hope it won't interfere too much. It doesn't rain here often, but when it does, it really comes down. Please don't hesitate to ask me to repeat myself if it gets too crazy over here."

"Don't worry, we won't," the older man said, straightening a stack of papers in his hands by tapping them on the desk before him. "I'm Agent Schloss; my partner here is Agent Robb. On behalf of the U.S. government, I'd like to thank you for agreeing to speak with us today, Mister

Sonata." Evidently satisfied with the papers' alignment, he handed the stack to his younger accomplice sitting silently by his side.

"Sanada," Kenji corrected. "With a d, not a t."

Immediately, he cursed himself for reflexively correcting the agent's pronunciation. What did it matter if he said their name wrong? After this conversation, he'd never see the man again, fate willing. Better to keep on their good side and keep his mouth shut.

"Yes, of course—Mister Sanada," Schloss said, already sounding irritated. "Anyway, we have some questions we'd like to ask you about your brother today."

"Absolutely," Kenji replied. "I'm happy to do so. Though I can't imagine that anything we've ever talked about would be of any interest to the U.S. government."

"You let us decide what's of interest to the government," cut in the younger agent. Robb, that was his name. "You just answer our questions fully and honestly, if you don't mind, Mr. Sanada," Robb said, overenunciating the d of Kenji's surname theatrically.

"Er, yes—of c-course," Kenji stuttered, shaken.

Schloss shot his partner a look before continuing. "Thank you, sir. Now, your brother is Kenta Sanada, age thirty, born there in San Diego. Is that correct?"

"Yes," Kenji said.

Robb held up an eight-by-ten photo, slightly blurry but clearly readable. It looked like a blowup from a security camera. "And you can confirm this is him?"

Kenji nodded. "I can," he said. "That's him. Where is that picture from?"

"As I said, sir, we'll ask the questions," Robb said, sliding the photo on the bottom of his stack.

"Now, Mr. Sanada," Schloss said, "according to our

sources you and your brother have historically not been the closest of siblings. Is that true?"

"I'm not sure who your sources are," Kenji bristled. "But we're brothers two years apart, so yes, we have our fights. Even still today. But we have a lot of love for each other despite our differences."

"I'm sure you do," Schloss said. "I didn't mean to imply otherwise. But you don't accompany him on his extracurricular activities."

"If by that you mean protesting the injustices of the world and striving for social equality, no, I don't. To be honest, we don't really talk about such things amongst ourselves in this family. But that doesn't mean I disagree with his opinions, necessarily."

"Again, I didn't mean to intimate that you do, Mister Sanada. I'm just trying to get answers to our questions."

"Sorry," Kenji said, the thunder cracking behind his head. "I'm just a little on edge." He swallowed the last of his hot chocolate, his throat still scratchy in its wake.

"Perfectly understandable," the agent said. "These are trying times for many people. Please don't feel the need to apologize. Now," he continued, "if you and your brother don't talk about the issues of the day, would you mind characterizing the tenor of your recent conversations? Say, over the past month or so."

"It's…a little embarrassing, to be honest. And I can't imagine it's anything relevant to your investigation."

"You let us—" Robb started up, before Schloss put a hand on his arm.

"Please," Schloss said. "Even if it seems trivial and silly, we just need the truth. And as far as potential embarrassment, let me assure you anything you say will be kept completely confidential."

"Well," Kenji began, looking to the wolfman on his

wall for confidence. "Lately, Kenta's been obsessed with this old movie, *The Tingler*."

His cheeks flushed. Schloss raised an eyebrow. Robb smirked.

"The Tingler, you say?" said Schloss.

"Yes, that's what it's called, believe it or not. It's not one of what you'd call the classic monster films," Kenji said, gesturing at the array of paraphernalia around him. "It was more an agglomeration of gimmicks than a cinematic triumph. A would-be theme park ride to give dumb kids a cheap thrill. It's more goofy than genuinely scary. Not a patch on the real stuff, like *Bride of Frankenstein* or Chaney's *Phantom of the Opera*."

"And yet your brother is obsessed with this film?"

"He is," Kenji sighed. "And he knows I know a lot about old movies, so naturally that's where our conversations have gone, of late. Honestly, it's just nice to have something to talk about that doesn't cause an argument," he admitted.

Schloss smiled wistfully. "I can sympathize. Family can be difficult sometimes. Even when you love them dearly."

"Yes. So if Kenta wants to go on about The Tingler, I tend to let him."

Robb leaned forward. "And what kinds of things does he say about this Tingler?"

"Well," he started, then paused, gathering his thoughts. "Before I go on, I want to emphasize that I can't find a single piece of evidence to corroborate any of the things he says." He gestured at an overstuffed bookcase to his right. "I have tons of books and magazines on the history of film, and horror films in particular. But this stuff Kenta is coming up with is way out of left field."

Robb nodded. "Understood. Please continue."

"Okay," Kenji gulped. "So, in the film, the Tingler is

like, this creepy centipede-looking thing that supposedly everyone has inside them, grafted to their spine or something. It's basically the physical manifestation of fear, something that causes people who are terrified to die if they can't express their fear through screaming."

Robb cocked his head. "Sounds screwy."

"It is," Kenji agreed. "But like I say, this was a goofy movie for kids. Anyway, Kenta says all this is symbolic. That the Tingler represents a genetic manipulation of humanity, that though the human race rose above the other animals due to our lack of fear of the future, of the unknown, at some point extreme reactions to fear were bred into us—all of us—by forces unnamed. Supposedly, this new sense of dread acts as a governor on our development, slowing the pace of evolution by keeping us frightened, both of each other and what is to come. The screaming represents inability to share our emotional terror with each other and thereby lessen it."

Robb looked over at his partner with a smile. "Sounds like your brother has spent a lot of time thinking about this goofy old movie."

"Yes. Too much, if you ask me," Kenji said, shifting uncomfortably in his chair.

"What else does he say about this Tingler?" Schloss asked, scribbling something on a piece of paper and sliding it before Robb.

Kenji wiped a bead of sweat from his forehead, wishing he had some water to relieve his parched throat. "That's...that's about it, really."

Behind him, lightning flashed; a second later, thunder cracked, louder than before. The storm was getting closer.

Schloss exchanged a glance with Agent Robb. "Hm," he intoned. "About it, you say?"

"Yes, I'm afraid so," Kenji answered.

"Mr. Sanada, I'm sorry to have put it to you like this," Schloss said, nothing about his voice conveying sorrow. "But you must trust that we're trying to avoid the worst of consequences for you and your family."

Kenji's eyebrows raised. "What do you mean?"

"We mean you need to tell us the full and complete truth about what your brother has talked to you about." Robb shuffled through the papers before him, held up an official-looking document to the camera. "This gives us the authority to bring your brother, Kenji Sanada, in for questioning at any time we see fit, as well as to detain anyone reasonably suspected of withholding information that could prove useful to our case. That means you, your brother…maybe even your mother and father. Of course, neither of us wants that to happen," he concluded, his words thick with insinuation.

"Kenta, you mean. I'm Kenji," he whispered, his constricted throat limiting his voice to a shade of what it had been. "My brother is Kenta."

Robb smiled, turned the paper back towards himself. "Why, you're right—this does read Kenji, not Kenta. Understandable, of course, as the names are so close. But still, there's no excuse for such insensitive clumsiness. My apologies, I'll have a new copy drawn up as soon as possible."

He set it aside, making no move to correct or annotate the erroneous name.

"Please," said Schloss. "Just tell us what he has told you. Nothing less, nothing more. Then we can leave you alone, and you can go back to your normal life as if none of this ever happened."

"Okay," Kenji said, defeated. "But it's complete nonsense. You see, the film's release combined a number of bizarre gimmicks: vibrating seat mechanisms, a blood-red color sequence in the middle of an otherwise black-and-white movie, even the first-ever mention of LSD in a mainstream context. Kenta contends that all of this was meant to get across ideas too complex for the civilization of the time."

"Too complex?"

"Yes. At the time, American society was at a religious peak, the atomic bomb was a recent development. On the whole, people didn't know much if anything about DNA, evolution, or the nature of fear, so they'd certainly never understand genetic manipulation on an evolutionary scale. Science was something to be feared, so they conveyed these ideas through the most prominent mainstream vehicle for fear: a shock horror movie. Kenta says the ultimate effect of these combined multimedia gimmicks was to implant the notion that the viewers' plane of reality is no more or less real than that depicted in the movie, particularly when the film exceeds the boundaries of the screen and that plane breaks through to them via multiple senses —sight, sound, touch."

"Sounds a bit far-fetched," Schloss said. "So these filmmakers and writers were getting this across to a bunch of kids looking for a cheap thrill? Why? It doesn't make sense."

"That's what I said," Kenji said. "Almost word for word. But he wouldn't accept that. He says these filmmakers, the writers, the actors were used by forces they weren't aware of —forces greater than them, greater than any of us, ancient forces working on geologic timeframes we can scarcely conceive—to make the movie and subconsciously warn humanity. Perhaps an opposing faction to those who implanted this fear into our DNA. These ideas were coded into this obscure independent exploitation film to get these concepts out to masses unequipped to understand them any other way, by introducing these concepts into the subconscious minds of the easily influenced adolescents who made up the audience of the time, knowing the more rational minds of adults—limited by fear—would never accept them. But as these kids grew up, these ideas might take root and develop. And that, Kenta says, is what happened to him when we watched The Tingler together as small children."

"You?" asked Schloss. "But surely you are much too young to have seen the movie in its original run."

"Yes," Kenji admitted. "But our parents saw it together as small children, growing up in Santa Barbara. They always maintained a fondness for it—said it helped bring them together—and they took us to a revival when we were around the same age they had been. They even had the seat buzzers, and a woman in the audience pretended to faint and was carried out on a stretcher midmovie. It made quite an impression on us."

"Hm," said Robb. "Well, that explains your brother's strange fixation on this movie, I suppose."

"Yes, that's it," Kenji anxiously agreed. "He's just way overthinking this whole thing. Clinging to something that brought us joy as children. But nothing I could say would get to him. He won't let go of this crazy notion."

"Interesting," Schloss said. "And that's really the whole of it?"

"Yes, sir," Kenji swore. "That's all the two of us talk about anymore. Frankly, it feels good to be able to tell someone else, it all seems so crazy."

"Well, Mr. Sonata—Sanada, excuse me once more," Schloss said. "I thank you for being so forthcoming with us. Agent Robb?"

"Yes, I agree," Robb said, straightening his papers and

handing them back to Schloss. "I think we have everything we need."

"Oh, okay," Kenji said, his heart beaming with relief. "What should I do if I need to get in touch with you?"

Robb smiled wryly. "That won't be an issue, Mister Sanada. You won't be hearing from us again."

Kenji struggled to mask his elation. "Great, that's great," he said. "I'm glad I was able to help."

"Goodbye, Mister Sanada," Schloss said, nodding to Robb. "Good luck to you and your family."

"And to you," Kenji said, but the connection to the agents had already closed, leaving him alone in his cozy den, looking at his own reflection in the empty screen of his laptop.

He sank back into his chair, feeling tension drain from his body as he let all the air in his lungs loose at once. It felt like he'd been subconsciously holding his breath for hours, waiting on judgment from on high. But the interview had come and gone, and the authorities were satisfied with what he'd told them.

He looked up. Ah, Count Dracula—you would never have suffered the inquisition of such fools so gladly. But though Kenji was no monster with powers beyond those of ordinary men, he'd deflected the attention of the threat at their gates for the moment. Time to celebrate with a drink, and maybe even a little weed to help loosen the stress and strain that had set into the muscles at the base of his spine.

As he rose from his seat, groaning with the effort, a deafening thundercrack sent him jolting back into his chair, sliding a foot across the floor in shock.

No, too close to be a thundercrack. And it came from the wrong direction: down, not up.

Shouting now, indistinct and threatening. A riot of footsteps, swarming through the floor below him.

His phone jangled with a stream of incoming texts. He pulled it from his pocket: its face was covered with messages from Kenta, all sent within the space of a few seconds.

"Kenji, what did you tell them?"

"Kenji, you didn't tell them about the Tingler, did you?"

"Did you? You did, didn't you???"

"Kenji, what did you do? The house is surrounded, Mom and Dad are in cuffs and shackles!!! They're breaking my door down right now!!"

"KENJI, WHAT HAVE YOU DONE??"

Thumbs flying, Kenji texted his brother back: "I'm sorry, I didn't know—please, please forgive me!! Are Mom and Dad all right?"

The message was delivered, but no response came back.

Heavy footfalls now, coming up the stairs towards him. Loud, throaty yelling.

Kenji sank to his knees, looking around at his precious collectibles. Even the powers of Frankenstein's monster would be no protection against the monster at the door now.

Tears flowed through his hands pressed to his eyes, and finally, he screamed.

Too late.

AN IDEAL FOR LIVING

I think everybody who's ever worked in a nursing home remembers the first time they lost a friend.

Mine was Randall Johnson, born January 1st, 1890. I met him my first day of work at Reed Retirement Center in hazy, industrial Roanoke, Pennsylvania. It was a small town supported by one factory and I was a young girl just out of school on my first job. I don't remember much else about my first day, but I recall every detail of my first encounter with Mr. Johnson.

I came into his room at 10:32 by the big red clock on his dresser. He turned away from the window, looked me up and down once, observing my fresh white uniform and long ash hair drawn back in a bun. He sniffed once, said, "Another one," and turned back to gazing listlessly out the window in his black bathrobe.

I changed the sheets on the bed, cleaned up a bit, and asked, "And how do you feel today, Mr. Johnson?" just the way they told us to.

Without turning from the window, he grunted, "The same as always."

That day was a November fifth, a Monday. I really started to realize something was different about Mr. Johnson the following weekend.

The center always organized special events for weekends: a party, a game, a movie, something. I don't recall what it was that weekend, but Mr. Johnson didn't want to go. He never went, he said.

"Why should I? I don't know those people. The only thing we have in common is that we're all old."

I turned to leave in exasperation, and I noticed the neat row of books on his shelf: twenty-six books, all bearing the name RANDALL JOHNSON on the spine beneath the title.

"You wrote all these?" I asked.

"Of course," he snapped. Then, "Have you ever heard of any of my books before?"

I had to admit that I hadn't.

"Of course not." he sighed. "No one ever has, not anymore."

I didn't know what to say, so I embarrassedly excused myself and left hurriedly, leaving him staring out his window at the leafless, withering tree on the west lawn.

A couple of weeks passed without incident, and Thanksgiving came and went. The day after, I realized that no one had come to see Mr. Johnson, and I asked him why that was when I got to his room in my rounds.

"They're all dead," he curtly replied.

"Everyone?" I asked incredulously.

"All of them. I'm the last alive of everyone I knew. The last of my generation of writers, for that matter."

"No children?"

"No wife to give me any."

"So why don't you try to socialize with the others here?"

"I have my work to keep me company." he said, gesturing to an ancient typewriter on a stand by the bed. "I'm nearly done with a new book—my first in twenty years. They don't do it like this anymore, you know," he confided, nearly beaming. "These young writers, they can't do it like we used to do. I'll show them how it's done."

I assured him that I was sure it was a good book, but warned him not to get his hopes up, just in case,

"No, you don't understand; this is my world now. This is all that's left. They'll publish it," he insisted.

The next day I helped him box the manuscript up and send it to his former publishing house in New York. After we dropped it off at the post office, he smiled a broader smile than I'd ever seen on his face.

"You'll see, Peggy. It's just like I used to do it. Everyone loved me back then. They'll love it."

It was titled *An Ocean of Mercy* and was heavier than an anvil, that was all I knew about it. He wouldn't let me read it. "Buy the book," he said when I asked.

All through December, he asked me every day if anything had come in the mail for him and every day he looked like a little boy who's been confined to his room when I had to tell him no, there wasn't.

Christmas came, sooner than either of us expected it to. I was the only person who got him anything: a foot massager. He gave me a copy of his first book, entitled *An Ideal for Living*. We were both pleased.

December 27th, a notice came for Mr. Johnson in the mail. As soon as I saw it, I snatched it and ran down to his room, ignoring my normal rounds.

"Is it here?" he asked when he saw the envelope in my hand.

I handed it to him, and he carefully pried it open with

trembling fingers. He withdrew the letter inside and unfolded it; I knew instantly by his face the letter was bad news. He threw it on the floor and turned away towards the window.

"Go away, please," he choked.

I picked the paper off the floor and quietly left. I read it silently in the hall:

Mr. Johnson:

We regret to inform you that we cannot endeavor to publish your submission, An Ocean of Mercy. It is the opinion of our reviewers that readers of today would find the style of the writing old-fashioned and uninteresting. Thank you for your submission.

Sincerely,

I crumpled the paper and tossed it into the incinerator.

The next few days Mr. Johnson lay listlessly in bed, rising only to go to the bathroom. He seemed to grow weaker with each passing hour, as if the mere act of existence was draining his spirit away.

Early morning December 31st, he died. I found him on my rounds, a grim look frozen on his face. Within eight hours, the room was emptied, Mr. Johnson's belongings boxed and packed in the basement of the center. They didn't take up much room.

The next night, I was watching television while reading *An Ideal for Living* when an entertainment news show came on. About midway through, they announced Randall's death. They gave a brief biography, then had this to say:

"Archer Books of New York today announced plans to reprint the complete catalog of Randall Johnson's books in special editions, culminating in the publication of a previously unreleased book, entitled *An Ocean of Mercy*. A statement issued by Archer today says, 'We feel that the works of Randall Johnson have a timeless appeal that today's readers will enjoy as much as his original audience did.'"

Timeless.

Timeless, they said.

I found a passage in *An Ideal for Living* that I liked a lot:

"Mike looked around, recognized nothing. He realized that the unfamiliar surroundings could hold great danger, so he decided to wait, one hand on his well-oiled pistol. After he was satisfied by the lack of noise, he went into the next room."

The tree on the west side of the center blossomed the next spring, too.

TELEMARKETING IN REVERSE

The dormitory certainly wasn't the ideal place to live, but it was in the path of least resistance and anyway we never considered it more than a temporary stopover, a base from which to launch further operations such as 'Operation: Secure Employment' and 'Objective: Apartment Rental'.

One semester was the allotted time slot in our lives assigned to the tiny cement cubicle on the third floor of Behringer Hall, a single room with a single bed and a desk, no kitchen or bathroom facilities, and a claustrophobic atmosphere that extended to my attitude towards the floor's other residents.

Friendships and alliances in a college dorm are always set at the beginning of the school year, when everyone is out of their element and needs a support system. By the middle of the year, those systems are already in place and a newcomer can only unbalance and threaten those tenuous, fragile alliances.

In any case, I had no interest in getting to know my new neighbors, who proved their common, useless banality to me with their every action, from the rah-rah sports paraphernalia they hung on the outsides of their doors to the tedious mainstream music they blasted at volumes calculated to draw other like-minded aficionados of the tedious out of their holes.

I'd just sit in my room and think to myself, "Really? Def Leppard? In 1991? Pearl Jam I could understand—it's shit, but at least it's current and aimed at this demographic—but Def Leppard? Amazing."

I suppose it was my blatant disinterest in bonding with my neighbors that fueled their interest in me. As far as I recall, I never did anything to provoke their interest, but it came unbidden nonetheless. No doubt if I had solicited their interest with a well-meaning flurry of self-introductions and small talk about the college football team, it would perversely have stated at nil.

The circumstances of our residence in the dorm put me in a unique position to vicariously eavesdrop on what was said about me. Only I was registered at the university, and we would certainly have been kicked out if the university housing authorities discovered that I had a non-student female living there, engaged or not. Each day, I would go off to class and Renée would go off to work at the bank, then after she returned I would go to work washing dishes while she sat silently in the room for fear of discovery.

Presumably, this allowed a lot of time for smoking and reading, but the thin walls of cheap university construction made conversations in adjacent rooms perfectly audible. Having little else to do, Renée naturally took to professional eavesdropping, and each day when I returned from work—after I turned on music in the room to prevent anyone else from eavesdropping on our conversation—I'd be treated to the litany of complaints leveled against me by people I barely met.

Most were predictable, I suppose: given the circumstances, it didn't take a detective to predict that some thought I was "strange" or "an asshole". Others rightly suspected "that woman" who was seen coming and going at all hours of living in the room, but apparently not enough to report it.

The complaint that cemented my conviction in the correctness of my actions was relayed to me after a particularly exhausting day of scraping dried cheese and half-eaten tacos off of hundreds of identical white plates; I knew none of my neighbors had real jobs, at most working a few grueling hours per week in the campus copy center or computer labs. Sticky with crud, smelling like bad Mexican food, I stumbled in, flipped on the Mekons' *Rock 'N' Roll*, and pried the caked, half-frozen military surplus jungle boots from my feet, only to be greeted with Renée's latest jewel: apparently there had been a three-way conversation next-door earlier in the evening involving the inhabitants of the rooms on either side of mine, as well as a floormate from down the hall. As relayed to me, the discussion (surely worthy of the Algonquin Round Table) went something like this:

Neighbor #1: "That guy's an asshole."
  Floormate: "Yeah, he's like, always smoking pot…"
  Neighbor #2: "…And he never shares it!"

This floored me. For some reason, this exchange struck me as offense enough to warrant plotting revenge.

I had already struck back against the first neighbor's blaring Def Leppard by playing noise guitar solos at deafening volume until I felt my message was adequately conveyed, but this called for something special.

That weekend, hometown favorite John Cougar Mellencamp played a concert in the football stadium that, according to the student newspaper, must've been attended by virtually every student on campus except me. It could have been a sidebar story: "Student Shuns Stadium Show: Feels 'Disconnected' and 'Disinterested' in Mass Phenomena, Say Experts."

No doubt my neighbors were among the throngs cheering Mellencamp's sub-Springsteen, sub-Seger stadium rock anthems while I reveled in the solitude of an empty campus.

I wasn't idle, though: the solitude afforded me the opportunity to work quickly and efficiently. I got Neighbor #2's phone number from the campus directory, grabbed my coin jar, and plugged ten dollars' worth of dimes and nickels into the photocopier in the dorm basement.

The next morning, the strains of "Rain On the Scarecrow" and "Jack and Diane" still ringing in their ears, the residents of Indiana University awoke to find the following message plastered on flyers all over campus: "John Cougar IU Concert Tapes — A+ quality right off the soundboard — only $7 — call Neighbor #2 at 855-XXXX anytime, 24 hours a day."

The phone began ringing early that morning, around seven a.m. It woke Neighbor #2 as well as me, but I didn't mind for once.

As soon as he hung up the phone, puzzled, it rang again almost immediately. This went on for maybe an hour until he finally unplugged his phone.

All weekend, whenever he dared to plug the cord back into the wall, the flood of interested inquiries into the availability of John Cougar concert tapes forced him to pull it again.

By Monday, the flooded had dwindled enough to allow him to reconnect the phone, this time with a new message on his answering machine: "Hi, this is Neighbor #2. If you're calling about John Cougar concert tapes, *I don't have any, and please stop calling me*. Otherwise, leave your name and number after the beep."

I smiled every time I heard it.

THE RUMBLE OF HEAT LIGHTNING ABOVE THE DEEP MIDWESTERN WOODS

First, the bass: steady, insistent, pulsing, like a racing heartbeat deep within the inner ear of a sprinter on the edge of hyperventilation.

Then the drums, a battalion of rumbling toms defying the orderliness of the bassline, rhythms crossing and intertwining and reweaving each other in a match of chess, or tag, or seduction.

High sharp stabbing guitar chords start in on the offbeats as if piped in from a neighboring planet, raining from the stratosphere, undeniable, blocky and thick—then absent again, changing the music by delineating what it is not, nesting in the negative space to burst through once more—but only when the proper, perfect moment comes around.

And finally, the point of contact and connection, the wail of a human voice operating at the fringes of its limits, enshrined atop an interlocking architecture designed to support and enhance its effects, intensifying and transliterating the meaning encoded in the lyrics well past the point of conscious comprehension.

Together and apart and fused as one they create a maelstrom of beauty, a shared peak experience resonant beyond the bounds of time and matter. The unmatchable spectacle of four consciousnesses in lockstep, magnifying and amplifying one another like robots merging in one of those old Japanese cartoons, the creation of a monolith towering above anything else on Earth at that precise moment. All are one, every sentience but a fragment of a universal unified whole, and past and future fall away and all that exists is here, now, the eternal living moment that is awareness, life, living.

And then the song ends, and Andrej Zelinsky is once again ensconced within a too-small room that stinks of stale beer and surly philistines, on his feet shouting his appreciation, palms pounding together with every erg of force he can muster from his ropy, tattooed forearms. His enthusiasm surpasses the rest of the audience put together, easily: 'smattering' would be a kind descriptor for the total amount of applause evoked by Ghosts of Midnight's set. Let alone the particularly abrasive number with which they pummeled the unappreciative crowd as their closer, if one can truly call the few audience members who bothered to show up early enough for the opening band a crowd.

No matter. Audiences throughout history have always been too dumb, too numb, too ill-informed, too self-absorbed to recognize eternal majesty even when it rattled the very air surrounding their feeble heads. Later, he thinks, later they will brag to acquaintances of being there, despite the fact that nothing of the experience itself lingers in their memories. That's really what their ticket price earns them: posting and boasting rights, the chance for random flakes of glitter to settle on their heads only as long as it takes to sparkle in the reflected limelight.

The between-band background music started up exactly from where it left off forty-five minutes before, filling the painful silence saturating the dry atmosphere. Andrej walked to the mixing desk, nodded to the chucklehead manning it—Dave or Don or Dan, one of those—before rechecking the multitrack recorder he'd painstakingly patched into the rudimentary soundboard. Still running, luckily—never a sure thing in a room full of half-sloshed, disinterested cattle—although one never knew how much of the ephemeral feeling of transcendence might have filtered past the microphones and transistors and microchips to be disassembled into ones and zeros for later reconstitution. The recording—he still wanted to call it tape, even though it hadn't been actual tape in a decade or more—was only what was left behind, after all, the souvenir of the musical performance, not the music itself. That only existed there and then, a time already past, never to come again. As far as anyone knew, anyway.

At least he'd been able to convince Ghosts of Midnight of the importance of bringing the recorder. Never mind that bands like the Western Warlocks, who hadn't even bothered to exist since the turn of the century, routinely sold thousands of albums a month simply by digging into their archives and polishing up the residue of some random night they'd rambled on in front of a bunch of similarly disinterested yokels. To a group like Ghosts of Midnight, each night was merely another in an unending string of similar nights, comparable only to the ideal to which they subconsciously aspired, memorable only for the many aspects in which their performance fell short of that platonic ideal.

But Andrej Zelinsky knew that what all bands thought of as an endlessly replenishable reservoir inevitably ran dry, sooner or later.

You never knew what might bring a band's productive period screeching to its end: sometimes it was drugs, sometimes it was betrayal, sometimes it was death. Those were the stories everybody wanted to hear. Usually it wasn't that dramatic, though. More often than not, it was just people not being able to get along in all the same tedious ways people in all walks of life fail to get along.

Sometimes a band would swap players in and out like the ship of Theseus and the spirit of the thing would keep shining through as if nothing ever changed; other times one member would look at another member the wrong way and it would never be the same again.

It didn't really matter to Andrej what it was that ended a group's creative life, though. It only mattered that it ended. And when that point came, he would be gone and on to work with another band, one still in the golden days within which they were effortlessly able to deliver transcendence and epiphany, the germinal pearl at the heart of the human musical experience.

Despite the paltry response from the malingering attendees at the Fourth Floor that sweaty July evening, Andrej knew Ghosts of Midnight still had plenty of juice left in them. It wasn't their fault they had been misbooked on a tour with an inappropriate headliner; most bands fell victim to the misguidance of self-serving management more than once over the course of their existence, particularly when out supporting their first or second albums. And as the road manager, his job was to keep the trains running on the rails, no matter the set of mismatched railcars he'd been stuck with.

Airways was a decent midtier act with a strong following guaranteed to pack the small clubs and even a few larger rooms—but their music was pure dance fluff, not much more than a strong beat and some repetitive slogans to shout over it. Not that there was anything wrong with music made just for dancing: some bands made music for listening, some bands made music for dancing. Some bands' music enticed a receptive audience to do both. And in that overlap, Andrej thought, was where epiphany lay.

But a certain type of band attracted a certain type of audience, and the audience for Airways was emphatically not there to listen. They drank a lot though, and drink sales were the only numbers club managers really gave a crap about.

By the fourth night of the tour, the pattern was well established: big weekend gigs interspersed with sparse weeknights. People went out to dance on the weekend, mostly, which at first had given Andrej hope that Ghosts' fans might make their presence known on the days between.

That hope had gone unfulfilled thus far, though, and that Tuesday evening in Bethlehem, Indiana, had been no different. If he'd been consulted, he could have told Ghosts' management that Bethlehem was practically a ghost town in summer, when all the college students were back home or off working internships. The townies with jobs had to work in the morning, so they weren't coming out on a Tuesday night to dance. And the townies without jobs didn't have the money to spend.

But management never asked him. Never mind that he had seen the inside of nearly every venue in North America twice over, never mind that he had seen and done and handled nearly everything one could see and do and be forced to confront out on the road. Management always thought they knew better than everyone else, and that never changed.

"Shitty night, huh," sighed Jesse Oyama, the lead

guitarist for Ghosts of Midnight, making his way unmolested to the mixing desk to stand by his road manager's side. "Oh well, can't win them all," Jesse said, nodding to chucklehead Dan—Doug?—as the soundman passed en route to swap the mic positions out and otherwise prepare the stage for the headliner's arrival.

"You never know," Andrej said. "Might be you reached a few people there. You never can tell exactly what's going on in people's heads. And don't forget, you get paid either way," Andrej reminded him, handing over a white envelope.

"Great," Jesse said, sarcasm dripping from his voice as he rifled morosely through the slim envelope of cash. "I'll chalk it up as a win then, I suppose."

Knowing there would be no ticket threshold bonuses coming no matter how long they waited, Andrej had collected their guarantee from the box office the moment they'd gone onstage that night. There would be no point to his waiting around until closing time, not that night; no more money would be made from this gig other than whatever paltry few dollars they soaked up at the merch table. Airways had negotiated a cut of the bar proceeds that night, but Ghosts were a long way from being able to make that kind of demand. Never mind that they barely had enough petty cash left in the tour fund to get them to the next town, let alone indulge in a hotel room.

Jesse stuck the folded envelope in the back pocket of his well-worn jeans. "Guess it's a good thing we saved that leftover pizza the promoter provided, greasy as it was."

"You've still got a few drink tickets, at least," Andrej said, his own stomach gurgling feebly in memory of the two thin slices he'd forced down hours before. They weren't even planning on sleeping in Bethlehem that night; getting a jump on their long drive to the next stop would save them from going further into the hole on lodging, even if Andrej could already feel his back aching in anticipation of the rough night to come.

But regardless of their deepening financial rut, sticking around the venue all night to put in face time with the promoter or watch Airways' always-identical set again wouldn't change the situation. Besides, he had shit to do.

"You planning on sticking around for the headliner?" Andrej asked.

Jesse shrugged. "Might as well. Got nothing better to do on a Tuesday night in the middle of nowhere. And as you say, we've got drink tickets to burn."

"Great," Andrej said. "Do me a favor, then—pass these on to the others, will you?" Andrej handed three identical envelopes to Jesse—sealed, but not indicated for specific band members. Ghosts of Midnight was old school, split everything equally among its membership. It was one of the things Andrej liked about them; such practices promoted intra-band unity and fellowship, and helped forestall the inevitable backbiting and nitpicking about finances that plagued every band that lasted long enough for its members to transition from delayed adolescence to something resembling adulthood.

Jesse nodded, accepting the envelopes. "Will do. You going to be back before loadout?"

"We'll see," he said. "If not, shortly thereafter. But let's say if I miss helping with the loadout, I'll take the first shift behind the wheel. Or even if I don't. Deal?"

"Sounds good to me, man," Jesse said. "Whatever keeps me out of the hot seat."

Andrej concurred. Jesse's driving wasn't so hot even when he was fully awake and hadn't been drinking.

"Okay, then," Andrej said. "Anything particular you guys need while I'm out and about?"

THE RUMBLE OF HEAT LIGHTNING ABOVE THE DEEP MIDWESTERN WOODS

Jesse shrugged. It was his default response to most inquiries, Andrej had noticed. He could see one of his bandmates eventually flipping out and attacking him over it, years down the line.

"You know me," Jesse said. "I'm easy."

That meant he didn't want to say what he wanted, not in concrete terms, not out loud. That meant like many musicians, what he really wanted was for someone to anticipate his needs, to be ready to meet them before Jesse himself even knew what he wanted.

A tall order for most. But Andrej had been a road manager for longer than Jesse had been a musician, longer even than Jesse had been out of puberty. The road was no place for the weak or fragile or easily rattled, and many musicians needed to be insulated from the grueling realities of what it really took to keep a band out on tour.

That was where Andrej came in. When money needed to be collected, he got it. When disasters needed to be ironed out, he fixed them. Basically, whatever needed to be done to make sure a show happened outside of actually getting up onstage and playing music, it was his job to get it done.

With the fun part of the evening concluded, Andrej headed out into the night to do just that.

The air was thick and damp out on the sidewalk outside the Fourth Floor, the evening air only a degree or two cooler than when they'd loaded in around six PM. That weird ozone smell that always heralded summer rain was present in full abundance; off in the distance, heat lightning rolled across the sky like rumbling flashbulbs from the black heavens.

The air remained weirdly still, as if waiting for some

silent signal to unleash the torrents of moisture wicked up into the cloudy summer sky. Across Bethlehem, bicyclists were cutting their plans short so as not to risk getting caught out in it, car windows were being rolled up and dogs were burrowing under porches in preparation for what was coming.

Andrej lit a joint he'd rolled up with the last of his stash and peered up at the clouds, wondering if he should shield his lighter as he did so. It would come, he knew. But not before his joint was finished.

Remembering which state they were in, he stepped off the curb and down the black-paved alleyway, leaning against the rear wall of the venue next to a dumpster, out of view of any cops who might be cruising by, hoping to pick up an easy public intoxication bust in between sets. It didn't matter that Andrej was invisible from the street; the siren smell of burning weed would draw the kind of people he was looking for, no matter the dankness of the alley.

Sure enough, within minutes a trio of raggedy-looking young men ambled down the alley towards him. The one leading the way had short brown hair and a full untrimmed beard; behind him trailed a dreadlocked redhead in a tie-dye that was more holes than shirt and a shaved-head punk in the classic leather-and-studs-even-in-the-summer-heat model of unwavering adherence to scene commandments. All three looked like they might have been students at one time, the kind of students who forgot the point of their time at school and lost themselves in vats of dime beer and bushels of cheap homegrown.

None of them looked like they were big fans of either Airways or Ghosts of Midnight, but Andrej knew you could never really tell what kind of people would get into a band.

At their last Sunday night gig, Ghosts had signed freshly purchased t-shirts for a pair of middle-aged administrative aides who claimed to have driven over four hours just for the band's opening set, and who were skipping Airways so they would have a chance of getting home before the sun came up. From the looks of these three, though, Andrej would have been surprised if they lived more than ten minutes away. In a town as small as Bethlehem, few enough things happened on any given Tuesday night that even people with zero interest in the bands might show up if they thought their primary interests might be in evidence.

Like drugs, and other people who liked drugs.

"What up, bro," the bearded kid on point said, raising his hand in what seemed an amiable wave.

Andrej nodded, sizing the group up in a moment. He didn't have anything to worry about from this lot, unless they pulled a gun out of nowhere—always a reasonable chance in that part of the country. But other than the minute amount of weed still in the burning joint, he had barely anything on him worth stealing. Not that they knew that.

"You're not from around here," Beardo said.

Andrej had heard those five words said to him in a lot of different ways, often as a threat. This time, though, it was a flat statement of obvious fact: in that town, in summer, everyone knew everyone else on sight. And Andrej wasn't one of them.

"Sure not," he confirmed. "Road manager by trade. Working with Ghosts of Midnight for the past few months. You here for the show?" Andrej asked.

The three men exchanged looks, as if they hadn't gotten their stories straight and wanted to make sure they were all on the same page.

"Eh," said the bearded one. "Not so much the show as the scene."

"There's fuck all to do in this town in summer," rasped the dreadlocked ginger. "Might as well come down to the Fourth Floor, see if anything's shaking, right?"

Andrej nodded. "I get you." He jerked his thumb over his shoulder towards the venue. "I just came from inside, so if you're looking for a crowd you can save your admission fee. Unless you all are big into dance music, that is."

"Pass," said the shaved-head punk, seemingly speaking for his compatriots.

"Mind if we get in on that?" asked the bearded one, nodding towards Andrej's pinched fingers.

"Not at all," Andrej said honestly, handing the inch of remaining joint over. "Last of my stash, though. We're scheduled to play Illinois soon, so no big. Was kind of hoping we'd run into something a little more interesting than cannabis, honestly, but no joy so far this tour."

Beardo and Dreadlocks exchanged a look as their bald friend inhaled from the end of the joint.

"We might know someone who could help out with that," Beardo said. "If you got money."

"I got money," Andrej assured him, holding his hand out. "Andrej."

"Marshall," Beardo said. "This is Sticky and Rafe," he added, indicating Dreadlocks and the shaved punk, respectively.

"Pleasure's all mine," Andrej said, stubbing the roached joint on the sole of his shoe and tossing it in the dumpster. "So what are we standing around here with our dicks in our hands for?"

He followed the trio up the street and around the corner to

a beaten-up gray-green four door Jeep, probably ten years old or more.

"Here you go," Marshall said, unlocking the vehicle and opening the driver side rear door wide.

Andrej stepped up and slid into place on the bench seat, but his left leg failed to follow: the heel of his shoe had gotten caught in the side running board step somehow.

He pulled, and felt a tearing, and his leg came free—leaving the heel jammed in the step.

"Shit," Andrej said, looking at the bottom of his shoe. "These aren't even that old."

"How did you even do that?" marveled the dreadlocked one Marshall had called Sticky, sliding beside him from the other side of the Jeep. "Bet you couldn't do it again for a million bucks."

"Probably not," Andrej said, leaning down to dislodge the detached heel, with difficulty.

"Fuck it," mumbled bald punk Rafe, looking back over his shoulder from the passenger side front—what Andrej's friends used to call the suicide seat back in the day. Rafe had already buckled up though. "You're on tour, good excuse to expense that shit, right? Get yourself a nice pair of Docs, something that'll last."

"Good idea," Andrej said, sticking the heel into his back pocket to reattach with superglue later. No sense trying to explain the limited finances of the kinds of tours an up-and-coming act like Ghosts got booked on. There was barely enough margin to expense legitimate costs like gas, food, and lodging. Clothing definitely fell outside that allowable sector, unless he could prove it was for some sort of onstage costuming. And Ghosts of Midnight wasn't the kind of band that wore costumes.

For reasons Andrej had never been able to understand,

though, everyone outside the music industry always thought anyone within the music industry either had plenty of money hidden away or was working some angle that gave them access to ready cash. The best he could figure was that the image portrayed in music videos seeped into the American subconscious so deeply that it was automatic: music equals cash. Beyond that, people simply wanted to believe it, wanted to go on thinking the musicians they had grown up idolizing all lived in mansions by the sea and skyscraping penthouses, not government-subsidized apartments and their relatives' spare rooms.

Sure, there were exceptions, most of which were household names. But overall, the rule was that unless you had some other means of support like independent wealth or family money, being a musician was a remarkably shitty way to earn a living.

Exacerbating the problem, of course, were the innumerable middlemen, agents, managers and the like that stood between musicians and what was rightfully theirs. As the visible, tangible face of the administrative side of the industry, Andrej had taken the brunt of many a musician's frustration, even when they knew he could do nothing to relieve it. Decisions were made far above his level, usually well before he came into the picture. But regardless, whenever there was a problem of any kind on the road, it was expected that Andrej would solve it, one way or another.

"All set?" said Beardo Marshall from the driver's seat, seemingly as much to himself as any of the other three men in the car. "All right, let's head," he added after receiving a few murmurs of assent, turning the engine over with an insufficiently muffled roar and an immediate blaring of loud, thumping hip-hop.

A lot of people wouldn't get into a car with three

random guys they just met, and most people shouldn't. Andrej had sized these three up instantly, though, and knew he had little to worry about, at least for the moment. If they were planning to jump him, they would have sat the beefier Rafe beside him instead of the rickety Sticky, who looked like he'd blow over in the wind that was coming. And they wouldn't have put their seat belts on; you needed to be able to move quickly and freely to get the jump on someone.

He kept his wits about him, though. He'd only inhaled enough weed to have something to exhale when passing the joint around, leaving most of it to his new friends. And they hadn't frisked him, so there was always the sheathed knife strapped to his calf if things took a dicey turn.

They roared off down the street, Marshall only remembering to turn the headlights on with a mumbled "Whoops" after passing a red pickup heading the opposite direction, flashing furiously at them.

"Dumbass," laughed Sticky, to Marshall's displeasure.

"Shut it," he shouted over the rumbling hip-hop. "Unless you want to find yourself walking home."

Evidently Sticky didn't want that. Rafe smirked at his friend being put in his place.

They went past a pair of intersections, stopped at a blinking red light, and were swiftly past the city limits, lightposts decreasing in frequency and the road beneath them getting more rudimentary with every mile they progressed. A few suburban subdivisions, a couple of McMansions, a convenience store strip mall, and then they were fully in the woods, tall trees stretching up into the black sky above them, the light from Marshall's Jeep making visible about fifty feet in front of them and ten on either side and behind the Jeep.

The road was paved but well rutted, twisting and

turning through the Indiana back hills. Marshall consulted neither his phone nor his friends as to their direction; all three seemed to know quite well where they were going. Andrej knew better than to ask; it would make him appear nervous, out of his element, not in control of the situation. Might put ideas into these guys' heads they wouldn't have had otherwise. Bad for everyone concerned.

Besides, it didn't really matter where they were going. It only mattered what happened when they got there.

Marshall slowed the Jeep, arced the vehicle right with a screech that crossfaded into the rocky racket of rural gravel, kicking up a cloud of dust as they rattled down an unmarked road, past a hand-painted sign reading 'NO TRESSPASSERS – THIS MEANS YOU!!!', coming to a halt outside a two-story cabin with six or seven vehicles parked outside, mostly beat-up pickup trucks aside from one incongruous late-model sedan.

The Jeep shut off, the hip-hop ceased, and the four men stepped out. Andrej couldn't hear any cars other than the highway off in the distance, only the chirp of thousands of bugs singing to each other from within the dense foliage. The air was thick with the acrid smell of burning wood, a few floating embers dancing from around the corner of the house, down a dirt path worn into the unlandscaped ground.

"This way," said Marshall, beckoning to Andrej, as if he couldn't figure out which way they were going. He hobbled after the other three, his missing heel and the uneven pathway making his gait awkwardly asymmetrical.

In back of the house, around a dozen people encircled a large fire pit made from cinder blocks, sipping from cans of domestic beer, passing joints, chattering and laughing as if they were the only ones in the world. Which they might as well be, as deep in the woods as they were.

"What up, Nash," Marshall said, waving to a burly man at the apex of the circle, closest to the back door of the house.

Cigarette dangling from his lips, Nash stood up, walked to them, clasped hands with Marshall and embraced him heartily.

"What up, brother," Nash said, nodding to Rafe and Sticky with obvious recognition but eschewing the hug he'd given Marshall.

He looked Andrej up and down, glanced to Marshall.

"Oh right," Marshall said, as if remembering his manners. "This is Andrej. He's the tour manager for that band Ghosts of Midnight. We ran into him down at the Fourth Floor."

"Road manager," Andrej said, extending his hand.

Nash took it, squeezed it firmly. His hand was rough and callused, but in different places than Andrej's own. "What's the difference?"

"Tour managers sit in an office and plan out the routing, the schedule, that kind of thing. I come out on the road and do all the shit work that actually requires getting your hands dirty."

Nash chuckled. "I hear you there," he said, and Andrej could feel Rafe and Sticky relax beside him. He guessed they didn't know Nash as well as Marshall, who clearly went way back with him, and might be nervous they'd be blamed if this encounter went south.

"Grab a beer from the cooler if you want," Nash said, reseating himself by the fire. "So what can I do you for this fine evening, gentlemen?" he asked.

Sticky and Rafe walked up by the house, helped themselves to the cooler; Marshall and Andrej sat on either side of Nash. Marshall glanced from side to side, as if checking to make sure no one around the fire was listening to his clandestine whispers. But it was obvious nobody gave a shit.

"Andrej here was asking if we knew anywhere to get our hands on anything interesting," Marshall said.

"And you naturally thought of me, huh? How flattering," Nash said, leaning in. "I did just get my hands on a really nice Glock thirty-eight. Forty-five caliber, which I know is confusing, but I didn't name it."

"Not that kind of interesting," Andrej said.

"Ah, okay," Nash said. "And exactly what kind of fun are we looking to get into this evening?"

"Looking for my friend Henry," Andrej said.

Nash frowned. "I don't fuck with Henry. Good times only at Casa de Nasha. I can do you some candy sticks at a good price since Marshall here vouched for you, but that's as far as I can do."

"Okay, I get it," Andrej said. "I'm sure it's good stuff, but it doesn't solve my problem."

"Sure," Nash said. "Sorry I can't help you."

"Me and Rafe wouldn't mind getting in on a couple of those candy sticks," Sticky said from behind them.

Nash looked to Marshall. "You?"

Marshall glanced to Andrej, his eyes plaintive and wide. "You sure?" he asked, clearly hoping that they could obtain a better discount with a bigger purchase. "It's good shit, bro, no doubt. Get you straight, guaranteed."

Andrej shrugged. "Can't do it, man," he said. "My call, I'd say sure. But it's not for me."

Nash nodded. "No harm, no foul," he said, beckoning the three men to follow him. "Grab yourself a beer, we'll be back in a minute."

Andrej ignored the invitation to get a drink a second time, watched the four men disappear into the house.

He settled back, staring at the fire, watching embers drift upwards into the cloudy black sky, pointedly ignoring the conversations from the others around the circle. For the most part, they paid him no attention either, save for a pair of yellow eyes fixed on him from across the fire pit. Andrej pretended not to notice, picking up a stick and poking idly at the ashes, blinking furiously when the smoke drifted in his direction.

He looked up again, and the yellow eyes were at his side. The face around them was sunken, unshaven, and sallow.

"Yo, man," the man said. "I saw you walking up. Something wrong with your leg?"

Andrej looked at him, down at his foot. "Nah, man," he said. "Just a busted shoe. Starting to ache like a motherfucker, I don't mind telling you."

"Cool, cool," the man said. "I got some pain management issues myself." He sat down beside Andrej, lowered his voice. "So did I hear right that you're looking for Henry?"

Andrej nodded. "That's right. That something you can help me out with?"

The yellow eyes flickered up to the house. "Might be could be," he said. "You paying?"

"I'm paying," Andrej said.

"You strapped?" the man with the yellow eyes asked.

Andrej shook his head. "Uh-uh," he said.

"Lift up your shirt," the man said.

Andrej did so.

"All right," the man said. "How much you looking for?"

"Whatever you got to sell, I'll take," Andrej said.

The yellow eyes lit up, envisioning a large payday. "You sure about that?"

Andrej nodded. "You got more product than I have cash on hand, I can get more tonight."

The man was practically salivating as he held his hand out to Andrej. "Reece," he said.

"Andrej," Andrej said, shaking the man's hand and then pulling himself to his feet, brushing the debris from his pants.

Reece glanced towards the bank of pickups by the house. "You got to say anything to your friends before taking off?"

Andrej glanced up at the house. A group of shadows flickered against the drawn shade of an upstairs bedroom; Andrej guessed they'd gotten into the candy sticks, lit one up so as not to have to share it around the fire.

"Nah," he said. "Let's head."

Reece's pickup stank of urine, like someone had passed out in it and pissed themselves, maybe multiple times. The floor was covered with fast food wrappers that rustled every time the truck took a turn, or accelerated, or braked, or did anything other than sit still.

They didn't do much sitting still. After rattling back down to the pavement, Reece steered them miles deeper into the woods, eventually turning off down a parallel pair of ruts that no one passing by would recognize as a road.

There was no music on, which suited Andrej fine. Reece looked like he was having enough difficulty keeping the truck pointed straight without unnecessary distractions. There was nothing but a radio in the dashboard anyway, and that far into nowhere the only stations they'd pick up would be religious or country, if any.

They drove on, making enough turns that Andrej was pretty certain they'd circled around on their own path at least once. But finally they came to a halt outside a rusting, decrepit mobile home up on blocks, stuck out in the middle of nowhere with a gas generator chugging away beside it.

"Show me what you got," Reece said suddenly, after not talking for the duration of the drive.

Andrej paused. The guy just now thought to check if he actually had cash?

He reached back to his back pocket, touched the heel of his broken shoe, reached back to his other pocket, pulled out his wallet, opened it up, rifled the contents.

"I got two hundred on me," he said. "Two twenty."

The sallow face fell further. "Thought you said you were looking for a big buy?"

"Might be, could be," Andrej said. "Like I said, whatever money you need, I can get. I need to see if what you got is worth the trip before wasting anyone's time."

Reece snorted. "You fucking guys in the music game," he said. "Fine, whatever. Wait here, then," he said, holding out his hand.

Now it was Andrej who snorted. "Fuck that," he said. "I don't know you like that. I let you drive me out here to bumfuck nowhere, it's not like I'm going anywhere. But I'm not handing over one damn dollar without laying eyes on what I'm paying for."

Reece's eyes widened and Andrej could see wheels turning. "So how you planning to pay if you want more than a couple benjamins worth?"

Andrej tapped his phone. "Crypto, bro. Or if the man really wants cash, we can make the trip back into town."

"Alright, whatever," Reece said, getting out of the truck.

Andrej followed, limping behind him up to the trailer.

The sound of Reece banging on the rattly door echoed across the hills, dying off instantly as the woods absorbed the sound.

"It's me," Reece shouted. "I got someone with me."

The latch unlocked and the door cracked slightly open, wide enough for an eye to peer out, the barrel of a gun a foot below it.

"This guy's looking to meet Henry," Reece said, and the gun barrel pointed at Andrej's chest while the eye looked Andrej up and down. "He's got two hundo in cash, but he says he's got crypto if it's good stuff."

The eye stopped peering and the door swung wide, though the gun remained. The man holding it was shaking back and forth a little more than Andrej would have liked for someone holding a presumably loaded weapon.

"I can do crypto," the man said, stepping aside and lowering the pistol to allow his guests entry.

The interior smelled like chemicals and misery. Most of what Andrej presumed was once a living space had been converted into a cooking lab, piled high with glass containers and plastic tubing and unlabeled gallon jugs, leaving only the dining area near the front of the mobile home uncluttered save only for the usual paraphernalia that came with heavy use: lighters, syringes, carbonized spoons.

The man with the gun eyed Andrej suspiciously from behind a furrowed brow and a bushy mustache that flowed seamlessly into his scraggly, unkempt beard, waving them to sit at the dining table.

Andrej slid onto the bench seat on one side of the table, felt a cold shudder creep up his back at the sight of a small cellophane bag filled with white powder. He picked it up, held it, examined it.

"This the product?" he asked. "Not sure if you heard, but I'm looking for a lot more than a stamp bag."

"That's mine," the man with the gun said, sliding into the seat opposite, left hand held out for Andrej, his right on the gun resting on the seat at his side. "I was just about to relax for a bit, if you want a taste before you decide how much you want."

Andrej placed the bag in the outstretched palm, the man's stained and mottled shirt only now registering with him as an old piece of King Mandom merch.

"I worked that tour," he blurted automatically, without thinking.

Reece scratched his arms, shifting from leg to leg agitatedly, eyeing the bag in his friend's hand.

The man glared up at him. "You mind? Trying to do some business here. Try to act professional even if you're not." The man closed his hand. "Go to the bathroom before you piss yourself dancing around like that."

"All right," Reece muttered, unable to tear his eyes from the man's closed fist.

The man sighed as the bathroom door latched. "Sorry about that. Boy has a one track mind. You were saying you worked for King Mandom back in the day?"

Andrej nodded. "Ayup. That last tour, and the one before it."

"Goddamn," the man said, peeling open the wrapped cellophane bag. "I saw them five shows before the end. Best concert of my life. That Bailey Kaeser was a motherfucker on the guitar. And what a voice! I was fifty rows back but you could have heard him scream loud and clear even without a microphone."

Andrej grimaced as a whiff of vinegar passed under his nose. "That was Bailey," he said. "Five shows before the end, that would have been Cincinnati? With Feral Child opening?"

The man nodded. "I didn't see them, though. I was partying in the parking lot right up until the Kings took the stage. Barely made it to my seat before they kicked into 'Dovetail'."

"I was there," Andrej said. "I didn't make the beginning of that show either, though."

He glanced to the bathroom door. Still no sign of Reece.

The man stuck a spoon into the cellophane bag, tapped a small amount of heroin onto the back of his hand, snorted it, and leaned back in his seat, eyes closed as he savored the rush of the drug entering his system.

"Ahh," he said, taking a moment to remember where he was and what they had been talking about. "You missed the beginning of that show? Damn shame. That was one for the ages."

"So I'm told," Andrej said dryly.

The man picked the bag of heroin back up, toyed with it. "So what were you up to instead of doing your job?" His tone was mocking, distanced from the reality of his words and the people they referred to.

"Oh, I was doing my job that night," Andrej said. "Matter of fact, about the time the band was kicking into 'Dovetail', I was in a place not too dissimilar from this."

The man's eyed widened. "No shit," he said, gesturing for Andrej to put his hand out for a bump. "That's a hell of a coincidence."

"Not really," Andrej said, struggling to keep his hand steady as waves of rage flooded his body. "I was out buying the heroin that Bailey needed to get through the rest of the night after that show."

"Damn," said the man, doling out a bump half as large

as the one he'd snorted up behind Andrej's knuckles. "That's hardcore."

"You're telling me," Andrej said. "Same shit ended up killing him dead a week later."

Before the man's drug-deadened reflexes could react, Andrej flipped the jot of powdered heroin into his furrowed face, causing the man to blink and flail as he grabbed for the grip of his pistol.

Andrej ducked beneath the table, slapping the gun away at the same time he pulled the knife strapped to his leg from its sheath, then plunged it into the man's neck.

The man's eyes went wide as what life he had left drained from him, gurgling in shock, clutching uselessly at his neck. His shirt no longer looked like King Mandom merch, but an indistinguishable red clot.

"Bailey would still be here if not for fuckers like you," Andrej said, swiping the cellophane bag off the table in disgust, sending powder flying everywhere as the flicker of light in the man's eyes died out and he slumped to the floor.

Swiftly, Andrej grabbed a sturdy-looking wooden chair, jammed it under the bathroom door handle. You could never tell how long heroin addicts would be in the bathroom, but it wouldn't do for him to be interrupted now.

First, he tore a piece of cloth from a dirty t-shirt, used it to pick up the gun, and tucked it into his belt. Then he washed his knife off in the kitchen sink, brushing the crevices carefully, making sure every bit of blood was off. After he was done, he dumped about a half-inch of bleach in the sink—addicts always had bleach around—and dropped the knife in there to soak while he proceeded about his rounds, tossing the mobile home.

It was the noise he made as he searched the trashed mobile home that roused Reece from whatever he'd been doing in the bathroom, which Andrej had assumed was more heroin.

The door shook and rattled as the man struggled to free himself.

"Hey!" Reece yelled, his voice getting louder and more panicked by the moment.

Andrej wrapped the piece of t-shirt around his hand, pointed the gun at the bathroom door, and kicked the chair out from under the knob.

"It's open," he shouted.

The door burst open and Reece drained through it, his gaze disconnected and glazed until alighting on the body bleeding out in a pool on the floor, then leaping to the gun pointed directly at him.

"Oh fuck," he whispered.

"That's right," Andrej said, keeping the barrel level at the man who had brought him up there, wanting to pull the trigger, knowing it was the safe thing, the smart thing to do. Somehow, though, he couldn't summon the anger within him.

"Give me your keys. And your phone," he demanded.

Reece did so. "Whatever you want, man," he said, his gaze continually jumping past Andrej to the corpse behind him.

"I was never here," Andrej said. "You never brought me here. Anyone asks, we left Nash's place around the same time, you gave me a lift as far as the highway, dropped me off. Then you picked up a hitchhiker who clobbered you over the head and then stole your truck. No one asks, you say nothing. Got it?"

Reece repeated the story back to him, a little garbled but close enough for jazz.

Andrej waved the gun barrel towards the door. "Get walking," he said.

Reece stepped down from the trailer, hands held in the air. "One problem with that story, man—the cops are going to want to see where I got whacked over the head by this hitchhiker."

"Good point," Andrej said, bringing the butt of the gun down on the back of Reece's skull.

He dragged Reece's limp form about fifteen yards, propping him up against a sturdy tree so he wouldn't swallow his tongue and tying his hands behind him with another strip of torn t-shirt. The schmuck would wake up in an hour or two to face a long walk back to anywhere, and by the time he managed to free himself and make his way back to civilization, they'd be well on their way to Illinois. Then it wouldn't matter even if he ran straight to the police to tell them all he knew, which an active heroin addict was extremely unlikely to do even in the worst of circumstances.

Andrej stepped back into the mobile home to resume his search, this time including the tiny bathroom. Starting at one end of the trailer and working his way to the other, he methodically poked under the sinks, ripped up the stained carpeting, opened all boxes and containers, and tore down the ceiling tiles.

When he was done, he'd piled up about twenty-four thousand dollars in cash, mostly in hundreds and twenties, nearly three pounds of heroin, and half again as much methamphetamine.

The cash he stuffed in a brown paper bag he'd found under the sink. The drugs he dumped out in the toilet.

He let the bleach run out of the sink, rinsed his knife off, dried and resheathed it. Then, holding his breath, he emptied all the acetone he'd found in his search on the floor of the trailer, dashing outside before letting the cool woodland air rush into his lungs.

He threw the gun back through the door of the mobile home, set the scrap of t-shirt alight, tossed it inside, where it landed atop the gun. Flames spread instantly, racing across the floor, up the walls, engulfing the body.

He threw Reece's phone deep into the woods, jumped into the truck, set the bag full of cash on the seat beside him, started the ignition. Something was definitely going to explode once the fire breached the other chemicals they had stashed in there, and he didn't want to be anywhere within range when that happened. With all those accelerants, the fire would burn fast and hot, leaving nothing behind but a burned-out metal shell and a pile of ashes. He did wonder if Reece would wake up when the explosions started, but not enough to stick around to see it.

Andrej wasn't stupid enough to drive around all night in a stolen car, of course. He'd wipe it down and ditch it in the woods before he got near any paved roads, walk to wherever he could call a rideshare to pick him up, tell the driver he passed out partying and his buddies ditched him. It wasn't that far off from the truth, he thought, not really.

He glanced at the clock on the dashboard, shook his head. There was no way he'd be back in time to help Ghosts with the loadout, not at this rate. Airways was probably close to wrapping up their set already.

Ah, well. He'd done his best. Even if he got back a half-hour later than planned, being able to sleep the next night in a real hotel room would cushion the band's complaints. None of them would doubt for a minute that Andrej had pulled out one of his trademark creative accounting solutions once more, not with full bellies and rested spines and a fully topped-off gas tank. And he was as wide awake as he'd ever been, more than ready to drive through the night, all the way across the Illinois border.

Hell, he thought. They could even afford to make a stop at a laundromat, send their clothes tumbling through enough suds to wash away all the tribulations they'd suffered over the past weeks. And maybe he would indulge in new shoes rather than supergluing his heel back in place.

He glanced up at the rearview mirror, wiped a speck of blood from his face. For a moment, he got a look into his own eyes, but he looked away before the image could register too deeply. Besides, the sky was going to break loose and pour down at any moment; the first flecks of rain were already speckling the filthy windshield.

Unwilling to sit alone with his own thoughts in the stranger's pickup anymore, he turned the radio on, spinning the dial until it landed on something, anything.

It ended up landing on country, all drawling slide guitars and midtempo laments. But for once, he found that was just fine with him.

AUTHOR'S NOTE

"Sometimes, People Just Have Things They Have to Do" was originally published by Short Story (Substack), February 15, 2023 (https://shortstory.substack.com/p/sometimes-people-just-have-things).

"Default Admin Credentials" was originally published by Creepy Podcast, August 13, 2023 (https://www.patreon.com/posts/8-13-2023-early-87536378).

"Dictated, Never Read" was originally published by Twenty-two Twenty-eight, June 30, 2023 (https://www.twentytwotwentyeight.com/single-post/fiction-dictated-never-read-by-a-j-payler).

"Sonata of Fear" was originally published October 26, 2022 (https://books2read.com/sonataoffear).

"An Ideal for Living" was written circa the turn of the millennium and constitutes the earliest surviving example of my short fiction writing. Was it written for a college class, perhaps? A possible magazine submission? A contest, maybe? Who knows? Long thought lost, it has been newly rescued from the archives and appears here for the first time.

Similarly, the text of the semiautobiographical "Telemarketing in Reverse" was written sometime in the mid-to-late nineties, then edited into this form, self-narrated and released as an audio recording in early 2004—an experimental one-off that I believe I just uploaded to an audio hosting service, posted on a web forum, and pretty much forgot about. This was years before independent authors could upload their own audiobooks to Audible and similar services for paid distribution (and I had a lot going on in my life at the time in any case, quite honestly) but I was already forming the vague notions of possibly someday being able to do what I do today—writing, narrating, and releasing my own fiction regularly—and this was my way of taking a stab at figuring out what that might sound like. I knew it was theoretically possible, as I already had voiceover experience from working as a broadcaster both in radio news and as a student DJ plus audio engineering training to boot, but no one that I was aware of at the time was actually doing anything like this. I suppose the fact that back then there was nothing much more to do with this recording after making it probably disincentivized me from continuing along these lines, but writing in general took a backseat to other concerns in my life for awhile so it was never really much of a consideration either way. This is the story's first publication since being posted on that website in summer of 2004; the audio version of this book includes that original twenty-year old recording, remastered to modern audiobook standards.

"The Rumble of Heat Lightning Above the Deep Midwestern Woods" was originally published February 2, 2024 (https://books2read.com/rumbleofheatlightning).

My deepest thanks to you, and all my readers.
-AJP, March 5 2024

ALSO BY A. J. PAYLER

NOVELS:

The Killing Song

World of Heroes: The Untold Secret Origin of the New Fighters

Lost In the Red

Terror Next Door

Bank Error In Your Favor

NONFICTION:

Trapped in This World: Culture on the Edge—The Omnibus of Pop Culture Writing

Encore: The Anthology of Music Writing

ALBUMS (AS AARON POEHLER):

20th Century Gold - Juvenilia

This Is My Revenge

You Had To Leave Your Mark

Dietrich

That Says It All

ABOUT A. J. PAYLER

Born to multiracial heritage in the same Honolulu hospital as Barack Obama, A. J. Payler earned his English degree from the University of Hawai'i, then eked out a living variously as a musician, technical writer, radio broadcaster, military contractor, audio engineer, comic store clerk, short order cook, press clipping agent, music journalist, and congressional archival assistant, shaking hands with everyone from Motörhead's Lemmy to Kurt Vonnegut along the way.

Since turning his attention to writing full-time, he has released the novels *The Killing Song*, *World of Heroes: The Untold Secret Origin of the New Fighters*, *Lost In the Red*, *Terror Next Door*, and *Bank Error In Your Favor*; his short writing has been published by Suspect, Twenty-Two Twenty-Eight, Flipside, Songwriter's Market, Creepy podcast, Cloaked Press, Short Story (Substack), EYE, Tailspins, Razorcake and more. He has also recorded and released several well-reviewed albums of original songs and opened for artists such as Silkworm and the Schizophonics, continuing to perform live as often as time permits.

He lives in Southern California with his family. Further detail on his writing and music is available via http://linktr.ee/ajpayler and http://ajpayler.com, where readers can get sign up for the A. J. Payler newsletter to hear about new releases and get free stories as they're released.

Visit ajpayler.com

"Wired playing, hooks, and above-average lyrics"
- JACK RABID (BIG TAKEOVER)

"Ambitious, soulful, paranoid, and analytical"
- JOHN BARGE (THE PANICS, WALKING RUINS, BC MAGAZINE)

"EXCEPTIONAL"
- BILL MEYER (MAGNET)

"One listen and I was sold... more than I could ask for!"
- FLIPSIDE

AARON POEHLER

AS FEATURED BY:

MAXIMUMROCKNROLL
HIGH TIMES
THE BIG TAKEOVER
FLIPSIDE
FIZZ ABSOLUTEPUNK.net
MAGNET Real Music Alternatives
RAZORCAKE **option**

STREAM AT SPOTIFY, APPLE, TIDAL, AMAZON, YOUTUBE, DEEZER...

songwhip.com/aaronpoehler

GET PAY-WHAT-YOU-WANT (FREE) DOWNLOADS AND STREAM AT:

aaronpoehler.bandcamp.com

Would you risk everything for one shot at immortality?

A. J. PAYLER

The Killing Song.

1996, the American Midwest:

Zach Coleman is beginning to suspect the nineties aren't all they're cracked up to be. His fledgling private investigation career is sinking fast, his band just broke up, and even his boring day job isn't paying off.

But when a chance audition with a long-lost, legendary rock star leads to the opportunity of a lifetime, will Zach turn his back on everything he's known and pray both his worlds don't burn down around his ears?

This thrilling narrative vividly resuscitates the smoke-saturated culture of the late nineties, smashes it up against the ruins of sixties radicalism, and gleefully deconstructs the remains into a thing of terrifying beauty.

books2read.com/thekillingsong

Visit **http://www.ajpayler.com** for information on currently available books and sign up for the **A. J. Payler newsletter** to hear about new releases and get free stories as they're released

Out of their element—and trapped beyond time!

A. J. PAYLER

LOST IN THE RED

Carson Adkins had no doubt he was born unlucky, especially after his college folded one semester before graduation—but he never expected to find himself caught deep in the heart of an uncharted land sheltered against the passage of time for decades!

Compelled to struggle for survival against terrifying odds and unfamiliar threats, Carson finds himself in a world he never expected, where every encounter forces him to confront deadly opponents and difficult truths.

When the alluring Delilah Munson joins his journey, Carson believes he may finally have discovered something worth fighting for—but as he soon discovers, this opaque backwoods jewel has her own agenda, not to mention the will to carry it out.

Torn between two worlds, can the fragile yet ever-growing attraction between a rural princess and a modern man far from home possibly survive in the face of a cataclysmic conflict far beyond the bounds of anything either could ever have imagined?

books2read.com/lostinthered

Visit **http://www.ajpayler.com** for information on currently available books and sign up for the **A. J. Payler newsletter** to hear about new releases and get free stories as they're released

QUARANTINED. ISOLATED. PARANOID. TRAPPED.

A. J. PAYLER

TERROR NEXT DOOR

Stuck at home with nowhere to run,
Kevin Tamura isn't holding up well under quarantine.
Exhausted from overwork and lack of sleep,
his sanity slips as society crumbles.

But what will he do to protect himself when
the greatest terror of all might be hiding right next door?

From the mind of A. J. Payler, author of LOST IN THE RED and THE KILLING SONG,
comes a story of a man pushed to the edge in a world that's ready to break.

Suffused with gripping tension, the explosive TERROR NEXT DOOR
is a thrilling suspense novel no reader will ever forget.

books2read.com/terrornextdoor

Visit **http://www.ajpayler.com**
for information on currently available
books and sign up for the **A. J. Payler
newsletter** to hear about new releases
and get free stories as they're released

They thought they'd hit the jackpot—but the jackpot hit back

A. J. Payler

BANK ERROR IN YOUR FAVOR

What would you do if enough money to solve all your problems fell in your lap?

Shane and Jewel have been hanging onto the edges of life by their fingernails for so long, they can't remember any other way of living.

When enough money to solve all their problems drops out of the sky, it seems like a windfall from heaven—but it might be the worst thing that could ever have happened.

Can love survive when money comes between lovers?

Caught between the criminal underground and the law, Shane and Jewel race towards freedom despite a parade of bizarre characters, secret plans, and hidden agendas standing between them and the life they so desperately need.

And worst of all, their greatest enemy of all might be looking back at them from the mirror—or right by their side.

books2read.com/bankerror

Visit **http://www.ajpayler.com** for information on currently available books and sign up for the **A. J. Payler newsletter** to hear about new releases and get free stories as they're released

DATE	ISSUED TO
OC 31 '68	
OC 10 '68	John Clifford
NO 8 '68	Jerry Larsen
FE 18 '69	Tom Hamilton

N 352 R4

06915